"Excuse me for asking, but what the hell are you doing?" Alex said.

"Trying to figure out where I'm going to sleep." Patti eyed the upholstered chair.

"How about the bed?" he suggested.

"Yes, but you're in it."

He considered for a moment. "I'll make you a deal. We'll go to sleep—in the same bed. Actually sleep. I promise not to do anything you don't want me to do, although I won't make any promises beyond that."

Suddenly Patti saw the humor of the situation. Here they were, a grown man and woman, primly bargaining over their sleeping arrangements.

"Sure, why not?" She kept her voice light. "As long as you're not the type who steals the covers."

"Hearts, yes; covers, no..."

Other Second Chance at Love books by
Jacqueline Topaz

SWEPT AWAY #249
RITES OF PASSION #258

Jacqueline Topaz *is a freelance reporter for the Associated Press, covering theater, dance, and music in Southern California. She also edits part-time for the* Register *in Santa Ana. After graduating from Brandeis University, she lived in Italy for a year on a playwriting fellowship. Among Jackie's loves: participating in her writers' group, going to the theater, and growing roses. She and her husband live in La Habra.*

Dear Reader:

October is here—and so are the newest SECOND CHANCE AT LOVE romances!

Kelly Adams has a special talent for endowing ordinary people with extraordinary warmth and appeal. In *Sunlight and Silver* (#292), she places such thoroughly likable characters in a dramatic love story set in America's heartland, on the Mississippi River. Riverboat captain Jacy Jones comes from a long line of women who know better than to trust high-handed men. Joshua Logan comes from a privileged background of wealth and breeding that's always set him apart. The battle of wills between these two *very* independent people sparks sensual shock waves that rival the currents in the ol' Miss!

Few writers create characters as warmly human and endearingly quirky as Jeanne Grant, winner of the Romance Writers of America's Silver Medallion award. In *Pink Satin* (#293), voluptuous lingerie consultant Greer Lothrop feels more comfortable playing the role of resident housemother to new neighbor Ryan McCullough than acting the femme fatale. But Ryan isn't about to accept chicken soup in lieu of tender loving kisses. Once again, Jeanne Grant demonstrates her superlative skill as a teller of love stories in a romance you'll treasure.

With the emotional honesty and sensitivity she is fast becoming beloved for, Romance Writers of America's Bronze Medallion winner Karen Keast touches our hearts with a story of forbidden love between divorcée Sarah Braden and her ex-husband's brother, cartoonist Cade Sterling. While she never shrinks from complex emotional issues, Karen dazzles us with her skillful use of male viewpoint, her lyrical prose—*and* her humor! I can't sing the praises of Karen Keast and *Forbidden Dream* (#294) loudly enough!

Love With a Proper Stranger (#295) by Christa Merlin is a powerful love story with an element of intrigue that will keep you breathlessly turning the pages. Anya Meredith doesn't think she's a candidate for a whirlwind romance, but Brady Durant teases and tantalizes her until she impulsively surrenders to passion. Yet when Brady is linked to a mystery surrounding an antique music box, Anya's trust in her lover is severely shaken. Don't miss this gripping romance written by the author of *Kisses Incognito* (#199).

For Anglophiles everywhere, Frances Davies's frolicsome pen creates an unabashedly romantic British drawing-room comedy (at times it's a little like a French bedroom farce, too!), complete with a cast of lovable eccentrics—including the hero, dazzling romance and mystery writer Andrew Wiswood. With witty one-liners and flights of sheer poetry, Frances whisks us to heather-covered Yorkshire and immerses us in whimsy. *Fortune's Darling* (#296) is a sophisticated, delectable romp.

In *Lucky in Love* (#297) Jacqueline Topaz once again creates a bright, breezy romance that will make you feel good all over. Cheerfully unconventional exercise instructor Patti Lyon is willing to bet she can take the starch out of staunch civic leader Alex Greene. But Patti's game-show winnings and laidback lifestyle don't convince Alex to support legalized gambling. In the bedroom he's mischievously eager to play games ... but elsewhere he intends to show her there's more to life than fun and frolic!

Until next month, enjoy! Warm wishes,

Ellen Edwards

Ellen Edwards, Senior Editor
SECOND CHANCE AT LOVE
The Berkley Publishing Group
200 Madison Avenue
New York, NY 10016

LUCKY IN LOVE

JACQUELINE TOPAZ

A SECOND CHANCE AT LOVE BOOK

LUCKY IN LOVE

First edition published October 1985

First printing

Printed in the United States of America

Second Chance at Love books are published by
The Berkley Publishing Group
200 Madison Avenue, New York, NY 10016

For Carolyn Vantress

- 1 -

"AND A-ONE! And a-two!" Patti Lyon stretched from the waist, turning her body smoothly to and fro. She wore a clinging black leotard, and her dark ponytail swished in time to the music.

Joints creaked audibly around the classroom. Senior Citizen Fitness wasn't exactly Jane Fonda's Workout, she reflected wryly.

"Oh, Miss Lyon, my arthritis is acting up." It was Zelda Roark, a widow in her late seventies who loved coming to class but hated exercising. "Maybe I'd better sit out the rest."

"Sure." Patti waved a hand airily toward one of the chairs along the side wall of the Community Center recreation room. There was no point in pushing discipline; the class was supposed to be fun.

Like life, she thought with a grin, catching sight of Zelda batting her gray eyelashes seductively at one of the men.

The recorded music zipped into "Staying Alive," and

Patti led the class in a sequence of kicks and turns. The twenty elderly ladies and two men followed with more animation than agility. They rent the air with blue-veined legs, knees cocked at odd angles, arms flailing madly.

By the time the hour was over, everyone looked flushed and merry. "It does my heart good just watching you," said Zelda from her chair. She gestured toward one of the men. "Don't you love his knobby knees? He asked me out last week, but I decided I'd rather stay home and watch Tom Selleck on TV."

Patti caught her breath and nodded, then remembered to glance at her watch.

Seven o'clock, and the city council meeting started in half an hour! She was cutting it close.

Quickly she gathered up her purse and tote bag. Calling out "See you Thursday!" to the room at large, she dashed out to her waiting MG convertible.

If she stepped on it, she would just have time to change in the ladies' room at City Hall. Irene would kill her if she was late.

Still, she allowed herself a moment's satisfaction about the class. It was rewarding to work with the elderly—almost without intending it, Patti had found herself teaching half a dozen such sessions per week in a variety of locations. Her paycheck—which came through the Citrus Grove Community College District's extension office—didn't cover more than the bare necessities of life, but she'd managed to fill in her budget with occasional game show winnings.

The older people were interesting and very kind-hearted, and usually she stayed after class to talk with them. But not tonight!

Ten minutes and a dozen frustrating red lights later, the little sports car screeched up in front of the Citrus Grove City Hall.

The low structure looked more like an office building

than a seat of government. The southern California community had a population under thirty thousand and reminded Patti of an old-fashioned small town, with its coffee shop where the old-timers gathered and the pharmacy where everyone knew Patti's name.

She grabbed her bag and darted up the steps. Like an Olympic sprinter, she whipped through the double doors, down the hall, and around a corner.

Oof! Someone tall and solid loomed in her path, and Patti careened right into him. With a thud, she found herself sitting on the linoleum floor, wondering what had hit her. Or rather, what she had hit.

"Are you all right?" The man bent over her, gray-green eyes peering into hers. The impact hadn't ruffled one lock of his clipped sandy hair, but he did look a bit flustered.

She had an impression of sensual strength as his fingers brushed her arm. Spiffy clothes, she thought, wondering why her heartbeat accelerated as she smelled the rich musk cologne that clung to his three-piece dark suit.

"I'm going to be late." Funny how her muscles wouldn't move. Maybe she'd caught Zelda Roark's arthritis.

"We could file a collision report with the police department, if you like," he teased. Perfect teeth set off a delightful smile, the highlight of a strong, tanned face, but there was appraisal in the lingering way he looked at her. "It's just across the street."

"I guess it was my fault," Patti admitted. "I was speeding. You see, I'm not dressed yet."

An interested gaze took in the skimpy leotard, which hugged her energy-whittled body and small pointed breasts. "So I see." An unfamiliar quiver of response ran through Patti. Why did she suddenly feel as if she weren't wearing anything at all?

This man struck an elemental chord in her. She couldn't make sense of it. He looked conservative—not her type at all—and there was no explanation for the primitive surge of heat that flushed her cheeks and made her want to learn more about him.

"Do you exercise?" she said.

"I beg your pardon?"

"Do you like to work out?" She'd been leading up to an explanation of why she was dressed this way, but now she saw from his disapproving expression that her remarks carried a double meaning.

"Not at City Hall," he said, a note of annoyance creeping into his voice. "May I help you up?"

She couldn't help feeling disappointed. So the man was simply a boring gray-flannel-suit type after all. Her hormones must have gone haywire, to make her react the way she had.

He looked so stiff and formal that Patti couldn't resist teasing him. "Are you sure you don't want to come down here with me? We could do calisthenics . . ."

"Not that I don't appreciate the offer, but—"

"Here." Suddenly inspired by an imp of mischief, she caught his outstretched hand and, instead of letting him pull her to her feet, tugged hard.

He tried to resist, but the freshly waxed floor and her unexpected assault proved too much for his balance. Down he came, with a sharp "Hey!" and landed half on top of her.

Instantly she became aware of him physically in a way that went beyond—or beneath– the expensive tailored suit. There was a real man in there, long of limb, hard of muscle, and short of temper.

His mouth was only inches from hers. The air between them vibrated, and for one crazy instant Patti thought the man was going to kiss her. Then a look of dismay showed in those changeable eyes, followed by a glint of anger. "This is hardly the appropriate place for a romantic tryst," he snapped.

"People spend too much of their lives worrying about doing the right thing at the right time," Patti responded. "Why don't you loosen up a bit?" She straightened out one leg and stretched along it to demonstrate.

The man arose, dusting off his slacks. "Do you plan to continue sitting there all night? You seemed to be in a tearing hurry a few minutes ago."

"Oh! Darn!" Patti jumped up. Her spontaneous approach to life frequently made a mess of her plans, and his distracting masculine presence hadn't helped at all. "I've got to go. Maybe we could do this again sometime. I teach an exercise class over at—"

"I belong to the racquetball club, thank you." He took one last look at her, at the heaving bosom and almost-bare hips. "And by the way, I don't wear my gym shorts to City Hall. A little respect for propriety isn't entirely a bad thing."

Then he was gone, leaving Patti fuming. Pompous man!

She stormed into the ladies' room and stripped off her leotard, replacing it with hand-embroidered white slacks and a matching Mexican-style top.

If there was anything she hated, it was conformity. She'd grown up with enough of that to last a lifetime.

Even now, she shuddered at the memory of private-school uniforms, stifling hours spent at etiquette classes, the irritated expression on her father's face whenever she dared to disagree with him.

What on earth had she been thinking of, trying to tell the man where she worked? Sure, he was built like a jock, but he had the mentality of a . . . a . . . corporation president, she decided, picking the most insulting epithet she could think of.

A few minutes later, her long dark hair brushed and

makeup in place, she returned to the entrance hall to find Irene Ramirez waiting for her.

Three-year-old Jennifer scampered across the hall. "Hi, Patti!"

Patti gave her neighbor's child a quick hug and turned to Irene. "I made it!"

"So I see." Irene smiled indulgently. "I know you never mean to be late, Patti, but it does seem to be a habit. Frankly, I'm impressed that you're here. Now—take a look outside."

Patti stuck her head out the double doors of City Hall. Parading across the steps were half a dozen people carrying banners that read "Poker, Si. Poker Face, No," and "Time Is Now! Poker in Citrus Grove!"

"Come on." Jennifer caught her hand, and together the three of them entered the council chambers.

They sat among a group of supporters. The proposal to permit poker parlors was the first item on the agenda, Patti noted with relief.

Thank goodness they wouldn't have to hang around until midnight. She had to be up early the next day to go to the final tryouts for another game show.

"There. That's Vice Mayor Greene, the one I told you about," Irene whispered. "He's going to be our strongest opposition."

Patti followed the pointing finger and stared in disbelief. It was the man from the hallway. Vice Mayor Greene—so that was who he was! Well, it figured, stuffy as he'd turned out to be. But still, what a waste of a gorgeous man!

Even from this distance, he radiated power and confidence, the very qualities that attracted most women—and put Patti on her guard.

And yet she thought she'd perceived something else during their brief contact—a hint of vulnerability, the potential for tenderness.

Nonsense. She must be fantasizing, trying to reconcile

his pulse-stirring effect on her body with his totally unacceptable personality.

She squinted at the nameplate. His first name was Alex. Named after Alexander the Great, no doubt.

He was talking to the city clerk, paying no attention to the audience. So he hadn't noticed her. But she was going to have to get up and speak! She'd promised Irene; besides, this was an issue she cared about.

Well, she'd just tough it out, that was all, Patti told herself with a mental shrug. So the man was sexy enough to short-circuit her nervous system. Who cared?

Besides, if she knew his type, he'd probably be twice as tough on her as anyone else, trying to prove to himself that he hadn't, for one fleeting instant, wanted to kiss her.

Irene had begun talking again, saying something about the Help Center fund-raising carnival next weekend. Patti roused from her reverie to hear her friend say, "Will you?"

"Sure," Patti said. Whatever Irene had proposed, she was willing to bet it was worthwhile. Patti strongly supported the Help Center, a project to combine Citrus Grove's community services to the elderly, poor, and handicapped in one central facility.

"Oh, and can you baby-sit Jennifer tomorrow night? You don't have a class, do you?"

"No, I'd enjoy it." Patti made a mental note. In her present confused state she was likely to meander off to the nearest shopping mall and forget everything.

Why did her gaze keep wandering back to that remote, commanding figure on the platform? Why did her skin tingle at the memory of his body pressing against hers on the floor? Maybe it was because she'd held herself aloof from men for too long, Patti conceded. But Alex Greene certainly wasn't the one she would make an exception for!

The mayor called the session to order. There followed

the invocation, the pledge of allegiance, and the consent calendar, all of which were disposed of within ten minutes.

Then the city manager began discussing the poker parlor proposal.

The parlors were legal in California, subject to local city council approval, and offered a potential source of revenue for the town. A number of citizens had expressed support, and several had contacted him in opposition, the city manager explained before turning the matter over to the the council members.

Alex spoke up. "Frankly, I'm opposed to the idea." Why hadn't she noticed before how rich and precise his voice was, or was that the effect of the microphone?

"May I ask why?" It was Councilwoman Franklin, a distinguished, middle-aged woman who was known to approve of the parlors.

"For two reasons." Alex still gave no sign of noticing Patti. "One, I think we're just asking—begging—for the criminal element to come in and take over the organization of these things. Second, poor people end up spending a disproportionate amount of money on gambling, money they need to buy food for their kids."

"But we have a state lottery in California," Mrs. Franklin observed.

"I was against that, too," Alex said.

The mayor suggested they ask for public comment, and the others agreed. Nervously, Patti went to stand behind three people in a line.

She caught Alex's stare as, finally, he recognized her. He gave a subtle nod at seeing her respectably dressed, but she sensed something else, too, a sensual awareness. The signals she was picking up from this man didn't jibe with the image he projected, or the reserve he'd shown in the hallway.

The speakers began, and she forced herself to pay attention.

The first man said he didn't like poker because gambling was a sin. He was followed by a woman who frequently drove to another city to play poker and would like to have it closer to home. The third speaker said he wanted to be sure teenagers wouldn't be allowed in the clubs.

It was Patti's turn.

"Mr. Mayor and ladies and gentlemen of the council." She thought the opening sounded dull, but Irene had insisted on it. "My name is Patti Lyon and I'm a gambler."

Everyone focused on her, heads turning, mouths dropping slightly open in surprise at her statement. You could have heard a pair of dice drop.

She felt Alex's gaze sweep over her again, exploring her slowly and thoroughly. Odd how sensitive she felt toward his reaction, even though she was trying hard to concentrate on her speech.

She wished she didn't have the uncomfortable feeling that he'd disagree with anything she said, however persuasive she might be.

"I'm not addicted, and I don't pour all my money into slot machines," Patti went on, nervously brushing aside a stray lock of hair. "A couple of years ago I got laid off from my job. I was a physical education teacher. Since I had time to spare, I auditioned for a game show, was accepted, and won twelve thousand dollars."

An interested murmur arose from the audience. Patti sneaked a glance at Alex, but it was impossible to read anything in his expression. Only a quirk of the mouth acknowledged her look, but it was enough to raise a tingle in Patti's lips at the memory of their close encounter on the floor. What if he had kissed her . . . ? She'd better not think about that now!

"I managed to get part-time work teaching exercise to senior citizens," she said. "Meanwhile, I've been on two other game shows. I won a microwave oven, a trip to Hawaii, and a lifetime supply of spray starch."

A chuckle greeted this remark, and Patti warmed to her subject.

"I also enter sweepstakes and contests. Some of you may know there's a newsletter that lists all of them, and I'm a fanatic. So far, I've won a five-thousand-dollar first prize and all sorts of other things, from a baseball cap to a freezer full of meat."

Mrs. Franklin was nodding in fascination. Alex looked grimly amused.

"You can't stop people from gambling," Patti went on. "They do it all the time. I do it. Practically everybody does, except maybe that gentleman who spoke first. The point is to regulate it and let the city show a profit. Why not? There are plenty of organizations in town that could use the money, like the new Help Center."

Enthusiastic applause accompanied her back to her seat. Patti hardly heard the last two speakers; her brain was whirling.

What had Alex thought of her? He'd maintained an inscrutable expression the entire time, as if she were some species of intelligent gnat that had spoken up against exterminators.

And yet she knew there was more than that between them, a physical electricity that transcended their mutual skepticism. Maybe it was just his political charisma. Maybe he reacted this way to every woman he met—but she doubted it.

It frightened her a little, to realize how intense he was, like a star drawing lesser bodies into its orbit. This was the kind of man she knew all too well—the sort who would consume her spirit and her happiness, too, if she let him. But she wouldn't, even if by some bizarre chance she did run into him again after tonight.

Patti knew her approach to life, her enthusiasm for taking risks, grew as much from experience as from her naturally buoyant personality. Taking chances made her feel free, as if she could breathe deeply at last. While growing up, she'd had recurrent dreams about suffocating. Maybe she'd just been born into the wrong family; her buoyant spirits had never fit in with their restrained propriety, no matter how hard she had tried.

Alex was speaking again, restating his opposition. Her comments had had about as much effect on him as a paper parasol would in trying to stop a hurricane.

How stuffy and proper he looked, sitting up there on the platform. Mentally she compared him to Mark, the man she'd been married to for seven months. What a catastrophe that had been, from start to finish. She should never have married Mark at all, but she'd been younger then and a lot more foolish. Fortunately, at twenty-six, she knew much better—didn't she?

Patti reflected for a moment. While Alex's stiff formality reminded her of Mark at this moment, there was a hint of wildness about Alex, too—an air of tension and wariness that Patti responded to instinctively. It was an undercurrent of primeval fire; she couldn't help wondering what would happen if it ever burst out into the open.

This was insanity. She'd never see him again, unless another council meeting was held on the issue of gambling. And then she and Alex would be squaring off at a distance of at least twenty feet. Just as they had done this time.

If he could ignore her, she could certainly return the favor, Patti decided, and folded her arms resolutely.

The mayor was speaking now, suggesting that they table the discussion until they'd had a chance to do more research. The other members agreed, and the council moved on to the next item on the agenda. The people who'd come to discuss the gambling issue left quietly.

"Well, phooey," muttered Irene as they crept out. "That means we have to come back here and do this all over again!"

Patti shuddered involuntarily. Despite confidence in her convictions, she didn't relish having to confront Alex Greene a second time. But she couldn't very well refuse to stand up for poker parlors when the revenue was so badly needed for social services.

"Patti?" Irene said. They were standing in the front hall, just inside the doors.

"I'm sorry. Wool-gathering." Patti grinned apologetically.

"Oh, that's all right. Listen, you'll need to be at the park Saturday morning around ten. Wear something pretty but not too suggestive. We don't want to give people the wrong idea."

Irene, pulled by Jennifer, was moving toward the door.

"The wrong idea about what?"

"You know. The auction." Jennifer stamped her foot, glaring at her mother. "Yes, sweetie, Mommy's coming, just a minute."

The little girl's face turned beet red, as if she couldn't bear another moment of frustration.

"What auction?" Patti asked.

Jennifer dropped her mother's hand in disgust and thumped across the hall and down the corridor. Irene kept an eye on her but made no effort to interfere.

"You weren't listening earlier, were you?" Irene sighed. "I knew it was too good to be true."

"What was?"

"You volunteered to be auctioned off as a slave for a weekend," she said. "Nothing sexual, of course."

"Too bad," Patti quipped. So that was what she'd agreed to when she wasn't paying attention! It served her right, she supposed. "Are other people doing it?"

"Yes, several."

"Well, okay. I won't go back on my word."

Jennifer had disappeared from sight. "I'll go check on her," Patti said quickly. She could tell Irene was annoyed with the child. It was a situation, Patti knew from experience, that could well result in an explosion of tempers between parent and child. Better for Patti to tease Jennifer out of her bad mood.

"Hey, kid, where'd you go?" She reached the turn in the hall and saw nothing. A prickle of concern ran up her spine.

Patti walked forward, checking for open doors. Suddenly, as she passed the water fountain, Jennifer jumped out and shouted with laughter at her startled response.

"Little scamp!" Patti bent and tickled the girl, being careful not to get carried away.

"Yours?" asked a masculine voice.

Patti looked up, startled, to see Alex. She hadn't even heard footsteps, but now she realized he'd come through a door to her right.

At close range, she realized afresh, he was even more devastating than in the council chamber. Maybe the effect was caused by the added play on her senses—his musk perfume, the heat that radiated from his body, the rich texture of his tanned skin.

"I seem to be peering up at you a lot," she commented from her crouched position. "Someday I'll have to even the score by seeing how you look lying down." Then she blushed. What was there about this man that gave all her words double meanings?

Unexpectedly, he chuckled. "You like pretending to be bold, don't you?"

"Oh? I had the idea I *was* pretty bold," Patti responded. "Anyway, what are you doing here?"

"We're taking a break," he said. "And you didn't answer my question." He knelt to inspect Jennifer gravely. "Is this your daughter?" His eyes were on Patti, as if a great deal hung on her response.

"No. My neighbor's. Aren't you, baby?" The little girl giggled and reached out to touch Alex's nose. It was a splendid nose, straight and finely chiseled.

Was he, the intimidating Alex Greene, trying to find

out if she was married? But why on earth? Patti had never met anyone in her life she had less in common with. Maybe she'd been right about his arrogance.

"So you're a professional gambler," he commented, straightening.

"You might say that." Patti tossed back her hair and stood up also. "Aren't we all? Life involves taking risks."

"Not with other people's welfare." He was dead serious now. "What you do, the way you live, is all very well for someone who has a teaching credential and can always go out and get a job."

"Patti? Did you find her?" It was Irene, coming down the hall. "Oh, hello, Mr. Greene. I'm Irene Ramirez."

"Mrs. Ramirez." He nodded politely. "I think I'd better be heading back inside. Since we banned smoking in the council chambers, we seem to take a lot of five-minute breaks."

Patti was glad to note that Alex didn't himself smoke—as an exercise instructor, she didn't approve of activities injurious to the health. But then, she chastised herself, it didn't matter, because she wasn't going to see Alex again, anyway.

She said good night to Irene and Jennifer and drove away, trying not to think about Alex Greene.

Home in her cluttered living room, she settled into the sofa to fill out three-by-five pieces of paper with her name, address, and telephone number; these were to mail to various sweepstakes.

But tonight's encounter had stirred up all sorts of memories, and she found it hard to concentrate.

Her hand cramping, Patti paused and gazed around the room. What would her family think of it, if they ever visited here? The rented house was tiny, only one bedroom, and the whole place was decorated in Early Garage Sale.

African batik fabrics were draped from rods over the windows, lending a bohemian air. The furniture was a mishmash assortment, chosen for comfort and cheapness. Books lay strewn about, and a candy dish overflowed with striped hard mints.

She thought of her parents' house in San Francisco, gables and narrow windows and high, echoing ceilings. It should have been enchanting, but instead it had felt like a prison.

Patti rested her chin on the palm of her hand. When she was a child, she'd imagined that someday she would be perfect. She'd win the Miss America contest, or graduate first in her class at Stanford, and magically her parents would approve of her.

Someday, Patti had thought, she would grow up and fit naturally into their world. She would—she thought—actually enjoy picking out subdued, expensive suits and stockings and spending her afternoons arranging with florists and caterers to put on elegant, at-home soirees.

It was painfully ironic that quite the opposite had happened. When she'd tried hardest to please them, she'd failed miserably. When her marriage ended, she sometimes thought they'd given up on her. Or perhaps she'd given up on them.

Since her divorce—it was almost eight years ago, now—her parents had kept contact rather superficial. Nobody ever talked about what they really thought, or felt. True, Patti saw her parents once or twice a year; last Christmas the whole family had gathered at her sister Ingrid's house in Denver. Yet her parents never seemed to know what to say to her; and when they did, their disapproval of her lifestyle showed all too clearly.

Sometimes she wondered if they were waiting for her to "come to her senses." At her most vulnerable moments she was afraid that someday she might find herself caught up again in that trap of trying endlessly to please, and endlessly failing.

She thought of Alex, kneeling to come face-to-face with Jennifer. Her own father would never have stooped that way. He'd always loomed over her. Yet in many ways Alex reminded her of her father. Was that why Alex had brought out her fighting instincts?

She flexed her hand to ease the stiffness from filling out contest entries. She'd better go to bed soon if she was going to look bright-eyed and enthusiastic at auditions for the game show *Lady Luck* tomorrow.

And then there was Saturday's auction. Slave for a weekend. With her luck she'd probably get "sold" to some rambunctious teenager and spend the weekend fighting off his adolescent advances.

Or maybe she'd get stuck with a compulsive housewife, who'd set Patti to scrubbing floors and ironing shirts for hours on end.

Her fantasies shifted to Alex Greene. He'd be horrified if he knew what she was up to. Getting herself auctioned off. Not appropriate . . .

For some perverse reason she hoped he'd be there. Just so she could see the expression on his face.

- 2 -

THE CALLBACK AUDITION for *Lady Luck* was held in a studio on Sunset Boulevard in Hollywood, almost an hour's drive northwest of Citrus Grove.

There was nothing glamorous about the room set aside for tryouts: simple wooden floors, straight-backed folding chairs, and a blackboard and a desk in front of the room.

Mentally, Patti sized up the other would-be contestants. There were about twenty people, most of them in their twenties and thirties, several wearing Air Force uniforms—from Edwards Air Force Base, or maybe Vandenberg. They all wore expressions of mingled eagerness and anxiety.

Through the door strode a trim woman in a business suit. "Hi. You all received callbacks, right?" Everyone nodded.

"Good." She perched on the edge of the desk, looking like a schoolteacher. "I'm Cheryl Walters. You're familiar with the rules of the game?" There were more nods. "Then let's play."

Luck was based on card games and trivia, both of which Patti had always been good at. But she knew the woman was looking for enthusiasm and personality as well as skill, so Patti made a point of calling out her answers loudly and smiling a lot.

Half an hour later the audition was over. "Thanks, everybody," Cheryl said. "We don't know how many of you we'll need. If you don't hear from us within two months, you can assume you didn't make it, but you're welcome to try again. I'm afraid we've had an awful lot of applicants, so I don't want to give you false hope. Naturally, we give preference to those of you who are visiting from out of town."

She looked up as a thin-faced young man with a clipped beard walked into the room and joined her at the front. "Hi, guys, I'm Bill," he said. "We thought you might be interested to know we're starting a new game show called *Double Luck*. It's similar to *Lady Luck,* but it's for couples."

An Air Force lieutenant raised his hand. "How do we apply for that?"

"Since you've already made the callbacks for *Lady,* we won't put you through another open audition," Bill said. "We're setting up a special screening session in a week or two, and we could meet with your partner briefly, then. Cheryl has the sign-up list, if you'd like us to call when we have the exact date and time."

Why not? Patti thought as she joined the line to sign up. She could probably scare up a partner—wouldn't it be fun to compete alongside one of her senior citizens? At any rate, she had nothing to lose, especially since the chances of getting on *Lady Luck* didn't sound too promising.

Patti walked thoughtfully out to her car, wondering if she'd be one of the lucky few who got called. She'd auditioned for half a dozen shows over the years but had actually appeared on only three.

Some networks had a three-show lifetime limit, but *Luck* was syndicated and therefore independent. She hoped she'd make it, or at least the new spin-off for couples. The income from her classes was barely enough to cover her basic expenses, with nothing left over for frills.

Irene brought Jennifer over at six-thirty that evening. "Paul and I will be home by ten at the latest," she assured Patti. "Just let her go to sleep whenever she's ready."

"I'm not tired!" the little girl proclaimed. "I'm going to stay up all night."

"Sure you will." Patti gave the child a hug and said to Irene, "She'll be out like a light by eight o'clock."

"I know." Irene lingered in the doorway. "What was that all about, between you and Alex Greene, anyway?"

"What was what all about?" Patti shot back.

"You two seemed to know each other. I was surprised."

"Oh, I ran into him in the hall earlier. Literally." Jennifer began galloping around the room, jumping on furniture, and Patti handed her a stuffed tiger to distract her.

"Did you notice the way he looked at you?" her neighbor continued. "I'd say he was definitely interested."

Patti laughed. "Interested in slitting my throat, maybe."

"Why? He's unattached, so I hear," Irene said. "And not hard to look at, either. It's time you found yourself a man, Patti Lyon."

"And got married?" she teased.

"Don't you want one of those?" Irene pointed to Jennifer, who was mauling the tiger. "On second thought, you can have this one."

"By the way." Patti hated to ask, but curiosity got the better of her. "What does Alex Greene do for a living, anyway?"

Irene tapped herself just below the eye.

"He's a Peeping Tom?"

Her friend chuckled. "No. He's president of Greene

Optics. They manufacture everything from sunglasses to laser technology. High tech, I guess they call it."

"I have heard of them, now that you mention it." So he was a corporation president, after all! Somehow the revelation didn't make her feel any better. "Enjoy yourself, wherever you're going," she said, covering her reaction.

"The movies. Paul's treating me to buttered popcorn. A rare thrill."

"Ciao."

Patti shooed her friend out and turned her attention to Jennifer, who wanted to hear *The Velveteen Rabbit* for the umpteenth time. With a sigh, Patti opened the book.

Later, with Jennifer asleep on her lap, she thought about what Irene had said.

Could Alex really be interested in her? The thought struck her as preposterous.

Of course, he might be attracted to her physically. Patti knew she was reasonably pretty, and he'd certainly gotten an eyeful of her body in that meager leotard.

At the memory her skin itched in an unfamiliar way. That moment when he'd fallen on top of her—his legs tangling with hers—his breath against her neck . . . Darn, why was she having this reaction to a man she hardly knew and didn't particularly like?

Well, one thing was certain. She wasn't going to let any stuffed shirt take over her life and bring her back to the straight and narrow. She'd worked too hard at establishing her independence to give it up for anyone.

On Saturday the lawn teemed with life in front of the Spanish-style building that was to serve as headquarters for the Help Center.

Women in brightly colored Mexican skirts and blouses staffed booths selling hot dogs, tacos, corn on the cob, and pita sandwiches—a real eclectic southern California mix, Patti reflected.

A mariachi band played with gusto on a small portable stage, the loud music adding to the confusion. Finally Patti spotted Irene selling raffle tickets.

"Hi." Patti displayed her own carefully chosen outfit, a silky Chinese sheath. "Do I look enough like a slave?"

Irene sighed. "I suppose I should be grateful you didn't wear a harem costume."

"I couldn't find one."

Jennifer scampered up amid a cluster of children. "Hi, Patti. Like my dress?" she spun around to show her ruffles and bows.

"You look beautiful," Patti said. The child took off at a dead run, shouting to her companions.

"The auction's in half an hour," Irene said. "Why don't you make yourself useful? Here." She tore off a string of raffle tickets. "They're three for a dollar."

"What's the prize?"

"There's a color TV, a five-speed bicycle, and dinner for two at La Maison Française."

"I'll take three dollars' worth." Patti produced her money.

"I meant for you to sell them."

"Okay. But first let me buy some. I can't miss a chance to gamble." She winked at Irene.

She then proceeded to talk several dozen people into contributing to the raffle as well. Patti was eager to see the Help Center get off to a healthy start.

Up until now, volunteer and community-supported services to the city's needy had lacked central coordination, resulting in inefficiency and duplication of effort. Then an elderly civic leader had died, leaving her home to be used as a center for such activities.

But the organization needed money, Patti knew. Endeavors like this could easily fall apart without sufficient funds and careful administration.

Fifteen minutes later she'd nearly sold the remaining tickets when she spotted Alex Greene standing with some of the other council members.

Although he stood several inches taller than his companions, it wasn't his height that struck her, but some inner force that burned keenly, even at this distance. The impact took her breath away.

Objectively, the man was handsome, true, but Patti had never been a sucker for good looks. No, there was something else about him, something that hit her almost like a physical blow—a fierce manliness that seemed to radiate from his very being.

Then he turned and caught sight of her. His gray-green eyes widened slightly and he gave a slow nod—of recognition? Or of appreciation for the dress, which suddenly felt much too brazen?

Not about to let herself be intimidated, Patti strode boldly toward the council members and launched into her spiel. "I wouldn't want to lead you good folks into sin, but how about buying some raffle tickets to benefit the Help Center?"

"Sure." Mrs. Franklin purchased five dollars' worth, and the mayor followed suit.

Patti planted herself directly in front of Alex. "Now, Mr. Vice Mayor, you can't truly believe this organization is controlled by the Mafia. And you can hardly call yourself one of the poor and downtrodden."

"Salesmanship by guilt," he observed, drawing out his wallet. "Very well, Miss—Lyon, isn't it?"

His eyes probed into hers, transfixing her. For a moment Patti felt like a butterfly pinned to a board.

She knew instinctively that they would dance well together, their bodies responding, always fully aware of each others' smallest movement. There was that kind of electricity between them.

"Well, thanks," she said, accepting his five-dollar bill and handing over the tickets. "But are you sure you want to support gambling? That's what a raffle is, after all."

His eyes played over her lazily and he took his time in answering. "Legally, they're required to give you a free ticket if you ask for it. Did you know that?"

"Yes," she said. "But nobody ever asks."

He nodded. "Well, I suppose I would be concerned if there were dozens of raffles going on all the time, but there aren't enough to cause serious problems. Now, how about something to drink?"

Alex's colleagues had moved away to shake hands with constituents. The realization that she was alone with him worked strange tricks on Patti's knees, which had always been perfectly sturdy and dependable up till now.

"You can get something at that stand over there." She hoped he wouldn't hear the tremor in her voice.

"No, I meant—I'll buy you something to drink."

He was standing so close that Patti could measure his height by her own. A good five inches above her five-foot-eight-inch frame, she estimated. Weight, maybe 200 pounds, well distributed. Age—hmm—thirty-two or thirty-three.

Her nerve endings twitched, imagining the feel of his length against her own, her arms around his neck . . .

Quickly Patti took a step backward. "I've, uh, got to get ready for the auction," she said.

"Auction?"

"They're auctioning off people—I mean, services. You know—hairstyling, cooking, that kind of thing. I'm one of the volunteers."

He seemed unwilling to let her get away. "Are you offering exercise lessons? On the floor at City Hall, perhaps?"

"Only for men in three-piece suits." Even to herself, Patti sounded breathless. She must get a grip on her emotions. Or possibly she was coming down with the flu.

"I don't mind exercising on the floor, and I've got

lots of three-piece suits," Alex said. "I'd like to take you up on it, if we can find an appropriate place."

It was the word *appropriate* that saved her. The man might be fun to flirt with, but he was a conformist at heart. "I'm sorry, I only seduce men in public places," Patti retorted. "Now, if you'll excuse me?"

She hurried away without waiting for an answer. If they could find a more appropriate place, indeed!

Then, suddenly, Patti began to giggle. Why on earth was she getting so upset? The whole situation was ridiculous.

She all but forgot the incident a few minutes later as spasms of nervousness attacked. Along with half a dozen other citizens of various ages, she took her place in a row of folding chairs behind the stage, waiting to be auctioned off.

On the block at the moment was a hefty woman guaranteed to clean your house from top to bottom. For a weekend—two eight-hour days—worth of work, she went for a modest one hundred dollars.

Patti stared nervously into the crowd gathered around the front of the stage. The council members were there, smiling and applauding. Naturally, they all showed up at public functions like this.

There were other faces she knew, and a lot she didn't. Until now she hadn't seriously thought about what she was getting herself into.

Finally she heard the announcer call her name. Shakily, Patti managed to mount the three steps to the stage. Everyone stared at her, and she felt like a denizen of the zoo. Or a stripper waiting to perform.

Why had she decided to wear this suggestive dress? She should have picked jeans and a smock. A burlap bag would have been even better.

"This young lady is an exercise instructor who can whip you into shape in the course of a weekend," the announcer was saying. "She's also an experienced babysitter and has appeared on three television game shows. She'll take you on at cards—no betting, of course. We wouldn't want to break the law." He winked at the mayor.

The bidding started at ten dollars. A young woman with three children wanted her, probably to baby-sit. Two college-age men in jogging suits also joined in, laughing and poking each other each time they made a bid. Oh, great. They'd probably have her clean the whole fraternity house and expect fringe benefits afterward.

The woman dropped out at seventy-five dollars, but one of the local storekeepers entered the contest. Most likely wants me to do his whole inventory, Patti thought morosely.

Her game-show skills came in handy. She managed to keep smiling as the bids rose.

"Do I hear a hundred and twenty dollars?" demanded the announcer. The college boys had made the last bid.

The storekeeper shook his head.

"Going once," said the man. "Going twice . . ."

"A hundred and twenty-five dollars!"

She couldn't see where the call had come from, but the voice was definitely male. Patti tried to peer through the crowd, but people were shifting around, preparing to bid on the next auction subject, a plumber.

Patti stepped dazedly to the ground. Had she really been auctioned off to a total stranger? Suppose he ordered her to do something, well, objectionable?

It wasn't until she approached the cashier's table that she saw Alex. He was standing there, writing out a check.

Impossible. But, clearly—true! Alex, the one man in Citrus Grove she most wanted to avoid, "owned" her for an entire weekend!

His voice. That deep masculine timbre—subconsciously she must have recognized it, but her conscious mind had protected her from the truth. Now she couldn't escape. She belonged to him, was his slave.

Come, come, chided her rational mind. This is only pretend. You've auctioned off your services—and they don't include anything illicit. He's much too proper for that, in any case.

Yet, watching his hand move firmly across the small slip of paper, she couldn't repress a shudder of mingled dread and anticipation.

A sideways look let her know that he was fully aware of her presence. In one instant he seemed to take in every detail from the delicate rosebud earrings to the color of her pantyhose.

"Why in heaven's name did you do that?" she asked, finding her voice disconcertingly hoarse.

"I couldn't let those lascivious college kids have you, could I?" he said. But his tone implied that a man of the world might do as he liked with her.

"Somehow I get the feeling you're more dangerous than they are," she moaned.

Taking her arm, Alex moved away from the cashier. "How could you doubt my charitable motives? I just wanted to help the center."

"Then you're not actually planning to use my services?"

Alex laughed. "I didn't say I was *that* charitable."

He led her toward one of the food stands. "Those hot dogs look overcooked. What do you say we go out to eat?"

Her fog clearing, Patti remembered something. "We can't start this weekend. I mean, it wouldn't be fair to you; Saturday's half over. We'll have to schedule it for another time." Relief surged through her: She'd won a reprieve.

"It's not often a man gets to purchase the woman of his dreams." Although the words were teasing, the look in Alex's eyes certainly wasn't. "You can't expect me to wait that long."

His hand touched her waist, lightly, and his breath soothed across her cheek. So close. Almost touching, but not quite. Patti thought her bones might melt.

"Maybe we could . . . start tomorrow, as the first day, and finish up the second day next weekend." At this rate she'd need the break to check herself into the cardiovascular unit at Citrus Grove Community Hospital, Patti reflected ruefully.

"That sounds like a good idea." His head was still bent close to hers. "But my offer stands. I'll treat you to lunch."

"Really, I . . . I'm sort of getting together with my friends . . ." Patti could never think of brilliant excuses on short notice, and she was a transparent liar.

"I've got an offer you can't refuse."

"What?"

"We'll flip for it. If I win, I take you out; if you win, I'll pay for your lunch and you can eat it with your friends." He produced a nickel. "Heads or tails?"

"Heads," she said.

He flipped. "Tails."

"Could I see an instant replay, please?" she asked suspiciously.

"Sorry." He placed her hand on the crook of his arm. "Might as well be gracious about it. I don't gamble much, but when I do, I always win."

"You'll have to teach me your technique," she muttered as he escorted her to his waiting car, a snappy new red Mustang.

"Where did you park?" He glanced around the lot, as if he could recognize her car instinctively. Maybe he expected one of those gaudy Volkswagen Beetles covered with slogans and pop art.

"Nowhere. I walked," she admitted.

"You live near here?"

"Obviously."

"You're right. Foolish question." He opened the door for her and even waited to shut it. What a gentleman. A gentleman pirate.

Patti wished she weren't enjoying his attentions so much. Some traitorous part of her soul missed the elegant restaurants, expensive clothes, and exquisite courtesy of her youth. Not that there was anything wrong with a bit of luxury, she mused, but she couldn't help linking that costly lifestyle with her parents' insistence on a place for everything and everything in its place.

In any event she would enjoy a leisurely lunch. Patti began to fantasize about shrimp in garlic butter sauce, or maybe a giant crab salad.

Her illusions were shattered a few minutes later when they pulled up to the take-out window at a fried chicken restaurant and he placed their order.

"This certainly puts those hot dogs to shame," she remarked sarcastically.

"Well, my original intention was something a bit more elevated, but I wasn't sure you'd be interested," Alex said.

"Oh, I'm rather fond of the finer things in life," Patti replied with what she intended to be sarcasm.

"Care to give me any examples?"

"I like caviar with my peanut butter," she said.

"Not exactly what I had in mind."

The waitress handed out their two boxes of chicken.

"Were you planning to eat these in the car?" Patti asked. "I may be offbeat, but I don't like grease spots on my dresses."

"Would you like to change?"

"I don't like grease on my blue jeans, either."

Alex laughed. "I guess I did miss the point, didn't I? Let me back up. A—we go to your house and you change. B—we have a picnic. It's such a beautiful day, I hate to waste it."

Someone pulled up behind them in the drive-in line and honked.

"I thought maybe we could sit here all day and consider our alternatives," Patti said. "Isn't that what city council members do? Maybe we could appoint a committee to decide where we should eat."

"All right, smart aleck." Alex shifted the car into gear and stepped on the gas. The surge of power pushed Patti against the back of her seat.

"Hot stuff," she said. "Can you make the tires squeal, too?"

Alex's mouth twitched but he kept a solemn expression. "By the way, where do you live?"

At Patti's insistence he stayed out in the car while she changed. Jeans didn't look sharp enough to her suddenly critical eye, so she decided on a casual caftan and sandals. Fortunately, October was usually a warm month in southern California, although the weather could shift abruptly.

"From China to Africa," Alex remarked as he helped her into the car. He actually got out and held the door again. For most guys once a day was enough. "Where did you grow up?"

"San Francisco." She snapped on her seat belt.

"That explains your affinity for international dress." He slid into his seat and turned toward her for a closer inspection. "Funny how that robe gives the impression of flowing loosely, whereas in fact it's quite revealing."

"Oh?" The word caught in her throat and she couldn't have said anything else to save her life.

His fingers stroked the fabric, brushing her leg underneath. Quivers of delight played along Patti's spine.

"You're extremely sensual, and you hardly seem aware of it," Alex murmured, half to himself. "All covered up, yet very much revealed."

His hand moved lightly up her leg, the thumb tracing her hip bone before passing along her waist. Patti could scarcely swallow, waiting for what came next.

"What an unusual woman you are." Alex's deep voice reverberated into her heart. "So open to life, to new experiences."

"Am I?" She was trying not to imagine how it would feel if he kissed her.

"I don't know you very well, and yet there's something that makes you stand out from all the other women I've ever met." His hands caressed her shoulders, and he turned her slightly to meet his eyes.

They were face to face, and Patti had no resistance left as his mouth descended.

Lips explored hers, firm and unhurried. Gradually her mouth parted and gave him access to the warm depths. Alex penetrated only to the tip of her tongue, as if fully confident that he could explore as far as he wanted, at his leisure.

Goaded beyond endurance, Patti caught him around the neck and deepened the kiss, probing him, urging him on. Soon she was lost in the hard mastery of his mouth.

And then, abruptly, he pulled away.

"I don't know what got into me," he said, breathing rapidly. "I don't usually act this way—certainly not in public."

She wanted to slap him. "I guess this isn't the 'appropriate place,' is it?" she snapped.

He started the car and headed toward the recently developed Town Park. "You forget I've got a position to maintain."

"Obviously the position is upright. With both feet on the floor." She knew she was overdoing this, but his sudden rejection hurt.

"Patti, this has nothing to do with you personally."

"Oh? Who does it have to do with, then?"

He laughed. "Me, I guess," he admitted ruefully.

In the warmth of his good humor, she didn't feel angry any more. And besides, why on earth had she wanted to go on kissing him? Time to change the subject. "Where are you from, Alex?"

"Boston. And don't tell me I don't have an accent. I got rid of it on purpose."

"Why?"

He stared straight ahead, navigating a tricky intersection. "I came out here to start over again. To be . . . on my own."

It was hard to imagine Alex as anything other than independent. A leader in Citrus Grove. What had his life been like in Boston, then?

She might have questioned him further, but they'd arrived at the park's picnic area. By the time they settled in with their chicken, she'd decided there was no point in raking up painful memories: for either of them.

An informal baseball game in the nearby diamond provided a pleasant background symphony of boyish shouts and ruled out any continuation of their embrace.

It felt odd, sitting here with Alex Greene in comradely silence, thinking about kissing him. He was her antagonist, after all.

Patti wanted to see poker parlors in Citrus Grove primarily because the income would help social services, not just because she enjoyed gambling. And clearly Alex was the main stumbling block in preventing this aim.

Yet she had to concede that he seemed genuinely concerned about the county's poor. He'd cited the danger of a needy family being deprived of its food money as one of his objections to gambling. For a man who was president of a corporation and probably had more money than he knew what to do with, he didn't seem to have lost touch with the hard realities of people's lives.

Had he come from a poor background, in Boston? Or did he simply have a natural sympathy for others?

There were a lot of things Patti found appealing about Alex, she admitted as she watched him spread honey on his biscuit and savor it.

For one thing he did know how to enjoy himself, and he could loosen up when he wanted to—like today.

He was also quick-witted enough to keep up with her sometimes sharp tongue, a trait that had plagued Patti during her younger years. She used to wonder why she couldn't just keep her mouth shut and smile demurely the way her sister Ingrid did, while thinking her own private thoughts. But no, Patti had always been outspoken, and she was delighted to find a man who wasn't daunted by it.

"A penny for your thoughts, or is that going to cost me another hundred and twenty-five dollars?" Alex asked.

"I was thinking about . . . my parents. They never took me on a picnic in the park." She hadn't meant to reveal that much—it just slipped out.

"Why not? San Francisco has beautiful parks."

"They probably never ate fried chicken either, come to think of it." Patti was trying to frame an answer when she was spared the effort.

A middle-aged couple walking a cocker spaniel nearby turned toward them. "Mr. Greene!" the man said. "I wanted to thank you for backing my zoning variance."

"It seemed reasonable to me, Mr. Andaro." Alex certainly wasn't trying to bask in his own self-importance, she thought, liking his modesty. And it awed her that he managed to remember the man's name. Patti had been known to call her best friends "Hey, you" on occasion.

"We needed to build a guest house for my mother," the woman explained to Patti as the dog sniffed around the base of the picnic table. "Some of the council members thought we were going to rent it out, but that isn't true. Otherwise, she'd have had to go into a rest home, and she would have hated that."

"I know." Patti's Tuesday and Friday morning fitness class was held at a convalescent home. The place was clean and well run, but most of the old folks longed to be back in their own homes.

"Well, we won't bother you any further. Just wanted to say thanks." The man shook Alex's hand, and the couple let the dog lead them away.

"That's what I like about being on the council," Alex said. "It gives you a chance to help people directly, in your own town."

"Oh, come on," said Patti. "Are you trying to tell me this isn't a stepping stone? I thought we'd be seeing 'Greene for Governor' signs any day."

He chuckled. "Afraid not. No, the next step in my life . . ." The words stopped abruptly.

"Well?" she said. "I'm waiting."

"The next step in my life is to take you home before you get tired of my company," Alex said. "We've got a long day tomorrow."

Patti felt a twinge of disappointment, which she ruthlessly suppressed. "Eight hours. That's all you paid for."

"Okay. Pick you up at one."

"Morning or afternoon?"

"Afternoon," he said. "Maybe we'll dine graciously . . . I realize you'd hate every minute of it, but you do belong to me, you know."

"I'll force myself." Patti hopped up to throw the remains of their picnic into the trash can. She kept her face averted to hide the conflicting emotions his remark stirred up. *You do belong to me*. He'd spoken the words so caressingly that she half wanted to yield, and her own vulnerability frightened her.

He drove her home and escorted her to the front door. Powerful arms closed around her, cradling.

"My little rebel," Alex murmured. "What is it about you that drives me crazy? I keep wanting to touch you, to hold you."

Patti drew her breath in sharply, not knowing what to say and yet feeling she ought to keep talking, to forestall any further developments. "I'm not . . . I mean, I wasn't aware—" His kiss cut off the rest of her reply.

His embrace was tender and yet commanding. Against her better instincts, she yielded to it, letting his tongue play soft games with hers while his fingers kneaded the muscles of her back. How easy it would be to let go, to take this man into her heart...

But only, of course, at the appropriate time and place, she reminded herself, and stepped away.

"I'll pick you up at one," Alex said, and then he was gone.

Patti finally admitted, as she closed the door behind her, that she was looking forward to tomorrow.

But only out of curiosity, of course.

- 3 -

Fresh from a good night's sleep, Patti woke up feeling strong enough to resist Rhett Butler himself. She maintained that illusion until early afternoon, when she answered the doorbell and saw Alex's warm smile.

For a minute they simply stood beaming at each other. Patti was too caught up in the unexpected delight of his nearness to remember to resist.

His hand brushed her waist as they walked out to the car. There was something protective about the simple gesture that made her feel cherished and safe.

"Where are we going?" Patti asked as she settled into her seat. The sun streamed in through the windshield, blazing its way from a warm morning to a hot afternoon.

"Church," Alex said.

That was the last place she would have guessed. Not that Alex didn't strike her as the churchgoing type—in fact, he did—but surely he hadn't paid a considerable sum of money just for the privilege of sitting beside her during a sermon. "Isn't it a little late for that? I mean, most services are over by now."

"It depends on what you mean by services," he responded cheerfully, putting the car into gear.

He looked crisp in yet another suit, this one made of light gray linen that did nothing to disguise the broad expanse of his shoulders or the well-defined musculature of his back.

Patti had to fight the urge to run her fingers along those enticing muscles. What happened to the self-confidence she'd experienced earlier that morning?

Now, sitting in the car, she was glad she'd decided to wear a blue wraparound skirt and a peasant blouse instead of jeans.

"Well, I'm at your disposal for the next eight hours," she said. "Provided you don't want anything illegal."

"Such as gambling?"

"I was thinking of other vices. The kind you're not allowed to pay for," she teased.

"I'm not in the habit of paying for them." He shot her a knowing look.

Even as she acknowledged his clever retort, Patti wondered how much truth there was behind his implication. A few discreet questions to Irene—which Irene had immediately seen through—had turned up the information that Alex was considered the town's most eligible bachelor. But, although he'd been seen out with a number of attractive women, he'd never settled down with any of them.

The car halted in front of Our Lady of the Flowers, Citrus Grove's impressive Catholic church. An assortment of people, all in their Sunday best, stood about chatting on the front lawn.

"Looks like we're too late," she said. "If you were a good Catholic, you'd have been at mass earlier."

"Nobody said anything about being Catholic," he teased. "Come on."

To her surprise they walked around the main part of the church and up a driveway toward a row of low-lying buildings that Patti guessed must be the parochial school. A few children chased each other around the entranceway.

"You want me to teach an exercise class?" she guessed. "You should have told me. I'm not dressed for it."

"You're batting zero today," Alex said, looking pleased with himself.

"Okay, I'll bite. What's going on?"

"For someone who sold her soul for the Help Center, you've got a lot to learn," he replied enigmatically.

They entered the building and proceeded down a corridor to the auditorium. Here, Patti noticed dozens of people sitting on rows of folding chairs while volunteers distributed boxes of food. She'd heard about the church's Free Food for the Poor program, but had never seen it in action before.

The room seemed to be full of children, dozens of them, dark-eyed and solemn, waiting uncomfortably at their parents' sides. They didn't look malnourished, but their clothes had that shiny, thin look of garments that have been washed too many times.

"Mr. Greene!" A nun, wearing a discreet headdress over a modest brown suit, bustled toward them. "What a pleasure to see you again."

"I wanted my friend to get acquainted with your operation," Alex said. "Sister Anna, this is Patti Lyon. Patti, Sister Anna."

The two women shook hands. "Do you do this every Sunday?" Patti asked.

Sister Anna nodded. "You'd never guess the degree of hunger that exists in Citrus Grove. It isn't visible, just looking around on the street. These people are proud, and they don't like being pitied."

"The children look so—serious," Patti said. Had she been so solemn, even in her unhappy years attending a rigid private school? She didn't think so. These youngsters looked as if the weight of the world rested on their shoulders.

"They know that how well they'll eat this week depends on the donations we've received," Anna said. "Most of them grow up before their time."

One girl in particular caught Patti's eye. She looked about sixteen, with dark hair and an attractive, heart-shaped face. But it was the fierceness of her expression that Patti noticed most.

The girl was bouncing a two-year-old on her lap and shushing a boisterous four-year-old while several other children squirmed on adjacent seats. The girl's jaw was tight, her eyes narrowed in anger, not at the children but, Patti guessed, at having to be there rather than out having fun like other teenagers.

Sister Anna noted Patti's gaze and said, "That's Rosa Nunez. She looks after her brothers and sisters—there are nine children altogether."

"How old is she? Sixteen?" Patti guessed, and the nun nodded. "That must be very difficult."

"Frankly, I'm a little worried about her," Sister Anna said. "Her mother tells me Rosa's been seeing a tough boy—he even belongs to a motorcycle gang." She shook her head as if to dismiss this unpleasant thought. "Would you like to meet her family?"

Patti nodded.

The nun escorted them across the room and introduced Patti and Alex to the Nunezes. In addition to the children, Patti met the parents and grandmother. Mr. Nunez was in a wheelchair, the result of a collision with an uninsured motorist, Sister Anna explained.

The grandmother looked frail, and her blue-veined hands held tightly to the aluminum bars of a walker. She barely nodded when Patti was introduced.

"She doesn't hear too well," Mrs. Nunez explained. A plump woman with a worried face, she clearly had her hands full taking care of her husband and mother-in-law. "We're so pleased to meet you, Mr. Vice Mayor."

Alex chatted with the family for a while, conversing in Spanish with Mr. Nunez about city services for the handicapped. He looked surprised when Patti joined in with the fluent Spanish she'd developed to help her work with the town's senior citizens.

The silent admiration in his expression warmed her, until, a moment later, he changed the subject abruptly.

"Sister Anna," Alex said. "You may have heard, there's a proposal in front of the council to legalize poker parlors in Citrus Grove. What do you think of it?"

Suddenly the situation came into focus. Now Patti knew why she'd been brought here. She suppressed a flash of resentment. After all, Alex was paying for her time.

"Well . . . I'm not opposed to a little gambling," Sister Anna said. "We sometimes have bingo games at church. But I don't like the idea that people can go in and bet large sums, and keep it up until they're broke."

"But shouldn't they have that choice?" Patti asked.

"Unfortunately, when you're so poor that there's hardly any chance of ever breaking free, people are easily tantalized by dreams of winning a fortune," Sister Anna said. "Before they know it, they've lost what little they had."

"Precisely the point I was making," said Alex. But he didn't look smug. Instead, a trace of sadness shadowed his eyes as he studied the Nunez children.

Rosa, who had been ignoring the adults, looked as if she wanted to escape, and yet she must know how desperately her family needed her, Patti thought.

"Hey." Patti addressed the youngsters. "Have any of you ever watched *Lady Luck* on television?"

A chorus of yeses greeted her. Even Rosa brightened.

"Well, I went down and auditioned to be on the show this week." Patti sat in a vacant chair. "Anybody want to try to beat me at the game?"

"All right." Rosa spoke for the first time. "Maybe I'll get lucky."

Patti pulled a miniature deck of cards from her purse. "You don't mind, do you?" she asked Sister Anna.

The nun smiled. "Not at all. In fact, I watch the show myself sometimes."

Patti glanced at Alex. He looked puzzled and also somewhat intrigued.

The cards were dealt, and Patti created a reasonable facsimile of the television game. As they played she amused the family by describing the other shows she'd been on.

"Did you win any trips?" asked Rosa, jiggling the two-year-old to make him stop fretting.

Patti nodded. "I went to Hawaii once, and another time to New York."

"Nothing like that ever happens to me," Rosa said, a trace of bitterness in her voice.

Wanting to reach out to the troubled teenager—with whom she strongly identified—yet afraid of coming on too strong, Patti pretended to be absorbed in the cards while considering how to respond. The other adults had resumed their own conversation.

"You know, a lot of people think card games are pure luck," Patti said.

"Aren't they?"

"Partly," she conceded. "But there's skill involved, too. It's the same as with everything else. People have a lot more control over their lives than they think they do."

"I don't." Rosa stared at the cards in her hand.

"Not entirely," Patti agreed. "But—"

"You don't know anything about my life," Rosa said.

"I guess not." Patti sighed. She'd hoped to make some kind of parallel between cards and life, but somehow she seemed to have failed dismally in her effort to reach the girl. Yet her empathy for Rosa wouldn't let her quit easily.

"When I was a teenager I felt kind of helpless, too, although my situation was a lot different from yours," Patti went on. "Eventually, I had to take control of things and make my own way in the world, and sometimes that looked like an impossible task."

"Oh, I can take care of myself," Rosa said proudly. "I've got my own life, but my parents don't understand."

A volunteer came by with packages for the Nunez family, and the ensuing commotion cut off any further chance at conversation. Patti wished she could talk with Rosa more, but it was clearly impossible under the circumstances.

After a flurry of good-byes, Patti and Alex stepped out into the dry, baking heat of the afternoon.

"You certainly have a way of making friends wherever you go," Alex said.

"I was worried about Rosa." Patti got into the car, and Alex swung into his seat and turned on the air-conditioning.

"Yes, I know." He nodded thoughtfully as he eased the car out of the parking lot. "So am I."

Patti regarded him thoughtfully. One minute, he was the stern city council member asking Sister Anna what she thought of a proposed ordinance. The next minute he was worrying about a troubled teenager. The more she got to know Alex, the more complex he seemed—and the better she liked him.

"Where are we going next?" she asked. "I'm afraid to guess."

"Que sera, sera," he hummed provocatively. "Whatever will be, will be."

"Now who's being profound?"

"I'm profoundly interested in going swimming, as a matter of fact. Did you bring a bathing suit?"

"Just a minute." Patti pretended to glance inside the neck of her blouse. "Nope, I forgot."

"Maybe I should check, just to make sure," he teased, feinting toward her.

"That'll cost you extra." She wished her body didn't tense automatically and her clothes didn't suddenly feel too tight as his shoulder brushed hers.

"It would be worth it."

"Vice Mayor Greene, isn't striptease illegal in this town?" It was amazing that she could get the words out. Did she sound a little breathy? Maybe he wouldn't notice.

"I just approved a variance." They pulled up in front of her house. "However, as long as we're here, you might as well go in and change."

Patti opened her door. "I'll just be a minute."

"Need any help?"

"Guard the curb for me, will you? It could be attacked by the dogs who run loose around here. We call them the Citrus Grove lawn fertilizer crew. By the way, why don't we have a leash law?"

Before he could answer, she'd made her escape into the house.

Despite her joking, Patti had to take several deep breaths to calm the rat-a-tat of her heartbeat. If only she weren't aware of Alex in an elemental physical way that transcended all her carefully maintained defenses.

Even her small joke about striptease was . . . provocative, somehow. She'd never before met a man who affected her this way, and she wasn't sure how to handle him.

Alex Greene was a unique man, no doubt about that, Patti reflected as she hung up her clothes and laid her three bathing suits on the bed. She had to admit he didn't seem to fit her stereotype of the businessman-politician.

She studied the flowered bikini she'd bought for the trip to Hawaii, the old black bikini she loved but which was showing a bit of wear, and her newest acquisition, a plunging-necklined, French-cut black suit with red, white and yellow strips up the sides. Impulsively, she put it on.

The matching skirt added a touch of modesty. But only a slight touch, she thought as she packed her skirt and blouse into a tote bag to take along.

It was a strange feeling, having to do exactly as Alex said—within reason—for the entire day.

Her instinct was to refuse to go swimming. Knowing the current that flowed between them, she feared what might result from such intimate contact.

But then, there would be lots of people around at the beach, if that was where they were going. Besides, she was old enough to handle any situation that might arise.

Patti twisted her hair up into a knot, leaving tendrils to curl around her cheeks. All set.

As it turned out, however, they weren't going to the beach.

"I like to swim, so I was delighted when I found a house with a pool," Alex explained as he steered her into the modern, airy home in the most expensive part of town. Located in a semiwild canyon area, it nestled among eucalyptus trees on a large, secluded lot.

Patti looked around, impressed in spite of herself. The place was clearly custom-designed, with lots of wood trim and banks of windows.

Inside, it was decorated in beige-gray tones with accents of rust and taupe, brightened by dozens of plants.

Alex gave her a tour, proudly pointing out how each of the four bedrooms opened on its own enclosed courtyard.

Light filtered airily through skylights, giving the place a relaxed atmosphere. Yet Patti couldn't help noting how tidy everything was—no rumpled bedspreads or dusty countertops. Not even a stray magazine or dog-eared paperback was in sight.

In the large wood-paneled den, Alex showed her his

collection of video- and audiocassette tapes, all neatly indexed and stored.

"You've got more equipment than a video store," she said, examining the video player, the laser disc player, the stereo, the tape deck, and the amplifier.

"I guess I do go a bit overboard." Alex grinned as he ran his hand through his hair. "That's what comes of being an engineer. I'm fascinated by this stuff."

"That doesn't explain the house," Patti said. "Why all this space? Are you planning to start a family or something?" As soon as the words were out, she blushed. She certainly didn't want him to think she was hinting at anything.

Alex waved her into an easy chair as he fixed wine coolers for them both. The den came equipped with a wet bar.

"One of these days I'd like to start a family," he said. "Most men in their early thirties are already married—some of them a couple of times—but I've always felt I should wait for the right woman. Not that I haven't had fun trying to find her."

"I was married once," Patti admitted. "For about seven months."

"Only seven months?" Alex handed her a drink and sank into a love seat.

"It was a mistake from the beginning." Rather to her surprise, she found she didn't mind discussing Mark with Alex. Something about the way he sat listening thoughtfully made her feel he would understand. "Mark was my father's protégé—my dad owns Golden State-San Francisco Enterprises. I guess you've heard of them."

That was a safe bet. Golden State-San Francisco Enterprises owned a range of companies, from a specialty food store chain to an airplane charter company.

Alex looked surprised. "Sure," he said. "You certainly don't live like the daughter of a millionaire."

"Well, that was what marrying Mark was all about,"

she admitted. "Trying to fit in. I thought I was in love with him, but really I was in love with the idea of finally belonging to my family. I was always the odd one out."

"I can't imagine why." His light note helped ease the sting of old memories.

"That's why I couldn't help identifying with Rosa—even though our backgrounds must seem completely opposite." She sipped at her drink, 7-Up blended with French Colombard wine, before continuing. "Only I didn't rebel. I kept trying to meet their standards, but I couldn't. Somehow I always managed to foul things up."

"How?" he asked.

"Well, I remember the time my sister, Ingrid, turned eleven and I was nine. She was really quiet, but I finally got her to confide in me that what she wanted most for her birthday was a puppy. So I got her one, from a kid I knew at school." Patti grimaced at the memory.

"What was wrong with that?" Alex asked.

"Well, I didn't understand that Ingrid's birthday party wasn't really for Ingrid, it was for my mother. So she could show off our new house to her friends. She had a beautiful catered lunch, and real clowns and jugglers to entertain, like a circus. Then I brought in the puppy and it went running through the house with its muddy paws . . . Well, you can imagine."

Patti closed her eyes for a moment in pain. Strange how the incident still had the power to hurt—the chaos, her mother's voice icy with anger, Ingrid's disappointment when the puppy was taken away.

Worst of all had been the comment she overheard later. She'd been trying to fall asleep when she heard her parents' voices down the hall. She'd caught a few random phrases, and then she heard her father say irritably, "What did you expect? You know how Patti is."

You know how Patti is. The words made it sound as if she were a hopeless case. The phrase had haunted her for years.

"Tell me about Mark," Alex said, bringing her out of her reverie.

"Oh, yes, Mark." She smiled ruefully. "Well, he was Daddy's second-in-command. Ingrid had gone off and quietly married a doctor, and I was left. Somehow everyone seemed to expect that Mark and I would get married, and after a while I expected it, too.

"We had a huge wedding, which my mother planned—I would have liked something casual, outdoors, with daffodils instead of roses—but I went along with everything."

She told him about the weeks that followed—the honeymoon that was cut short because of a business deal, the long evenings waiting for Mark to come home from the office, and then discovering they had nothing to talk about when he did.

Patti could still feel the stifling narrowness of that life. She'd given up on expressing opinions, because Mark belittled her when she did. And he objected to her closest friends from high school, so that although she still kept in touch with them, her weekends were spent socializing with his stuffy business friends.

Then came the morning she couldn't get out of bed. "I kept seeing the next fifty years stretched ahead of me, and I couldn't bear it," Patti said. "I wondered if it might help if I had a baby, but thank goodness I had the sense to realize I wasn't ready to be a parent yet. I need to grow up myself, first."

Across from her, Alex listened intently, his wine cooler scarcely touched.

"So I told Mark I wanted to go to college," she said. "He refused, point-blank. And my parents stood by him. They said I should devote myself to my marriage, at least for the first few years. My father told me I'd finally, for the first time in my life, taken on something worthwhile by marrying Mark, and I shouldn't make a mess of it by dabbling in what he called 'this self-fulfillment business.'"

"So you ended up divorcing not only your husband but, in a manner of speaking, your parents, too?" Alex asked.

"I never really thought about it that way, but yes," Patti said. "Oh, I see my parents from time to time, but we always feel—estranged. At least, I do. Of course, I did rebel for a while after my divorce. I dated a lot of hippie types while I was in college—I did finally make it there—but that was only temporary."

"At least your parents put you through school—or did they?" he said.

"I started out paying myself. I worked as a waitress. I'm convinced it was because they thought their friends would find out that they offered to pay." Patti's lips tightened at the memory. "I wanted to turn them down, but it would have been foolish, I guess. Anyway, I took their help."

"But you still make a point of being somewhat, shall we say, bohemian," Alex observed. "Isn't that a form of rebellion?"

"No, of course not." Patti heard the note of defiance in her tone, but decided it was justified. "I just like being spontaneous. Don't you ever get tired of doing everything right?"

Alex laughed, startled. "Do I do everything right? I'm flattered."

She smiled, too. "Well, not when it comes to poker parlors, but I meant—don't you get tired of always wearing the right clothes and having your house look like something out of *Better Homes and Gardens*?"

"Actually, no," he said.

"Don't you ever want to throw your clothes on the floor? Or cut up old magazines all over the coffee table?"

"Somehow I manage to resist the urge." He looked

amused. "I imagine a person can be quite creative without living in a whirlwind. My mother has always enjoyed painting—watercolors, mostly—but she keeps the house neat as a pin."

An image flashed into Patti's mind, of a neatly smock-clad lady with silvering hair, dabbling at an easel while a maid wiped up any droplets of water that spilled onto the hardwood floor.

Disappointment cut through her. Alex really didn't understand, did he? To him, creativity and self-expression were fine as long as they didn't interfere with a woman's basic housewifely duties, Patti thought.

"Did I say something wrong?" He was studying her expression.

"I was just wondering if that's all your mother did—keep house and paint," she said.

He smiled indulgently. "My mother was amazing. I've never known anyone like her. She could put together a charity luncheon in the morning, spend the afternoon organizing hospital volunteers, and find time to fix dinner herself."

So, he wasn't from a poor family after all—he was from a home more like hers. And what he had just described was his ideal wife—efficient, polished, respected in the community, and selfless, Patti thought.

Selfless—it could mean generous, but it also meant without a self. Before he could query her further, Patti offered, "Maybe we'd better go swimming before it gets too late."

He agreed, and they moved out onto the rear deck.

"You swim a lot?" she asked, regarding the large pool. The grounds around it were landscaped with clumps of calla lilies, orange and purple birds-of-paradise, and rosebushes in full bloom.

"Every morning. And you?"

"When I get the chance." Patti tossed her towel down on a chaise longue and removed her skirt. She turned to find Alex studying her with a thoroughness that brought back the first time they'd met, when she sprawled beneath him in the corridor.

"This was the most modest bathing suit I own," she admitted.

"I can't wait to see the others." He reached out boldly and traced the line of the suit, up high on her hip.

Heat prickled through Patti's body. It's only because I feel so vulnerable, standing here with so little on, she told herself. "Let's swim, shall we?"

"In a minute." His hand on her waist cut off her attempt to pull away. "I think I'm entitled to inspect you. To be sure you're the same woman I bid on."

"Don't you think we ought . . ."

The protest died as he bent and nibbled the curve of her throat. His tongue trailed scintillating moisture up to her chin, and then found its home in her mouth.

Fierce arms drew her close, and Patti could no longer fight the longing to stretch against him length for length. She reveled in the hardness of his chest against her soft breasts and the hair-roughened firmness of his legs against her velvety ones.

Their kiss deepened, matured, grew into a soul-enflaming rhapsody. Fingers played down her spine, tracing the bare skin to the edge of the fabric. Then he gripped her rounded bottom through the cloth, pulling her tight against him.

Her own body answered his, desire for desire. She wanted him. This man that she hardly knew somehow managed to fire her with unexplored passions.

But she must be careful. She couldn't, wouldn't let herself be swept away and lost.

Oh, how seductive he was. Sitting in his den a few minutes ago, she'd opened up to him in a way she hadn't done with any man before.

He touched a chord in her, an instinctive response. Maybe it was the overpoweringly masculine aura of the man. Or the way he took command of situations, just as her father had done. How lovely it would be to live with Alex and allow herself to be pampered...

And how suffocating. Just like living with her father. Just like her marriage to Mark. Patti stiffened, remembering those months of her marriage. She'd been sure her spirit was dying...

Alex lifted his head. "Sweetheart? What's wrong?"

"This is all happening too fast," she murmured, unwilling to reveal the depth of her susceptibility.

He hesitated, his breath coming raggedly, and then released her. "I challenge you to a race. I'll even give you a head start."

"But my hair!" She lifted a hand, to find that the pins still held it in place.

"I've got a blow-dryer," he said. "Besides, I have a feeling you look irresistible wet."

Dashing away without daring to look back, she dived into the pool. The water was heated, and the buoyancy eased her tensions.

A slight ripple marked Alex's entrance, and a second later he popped up nearby. "Ready?" he said.

Patti refused the offer of a head start. Agreeing to make four lengths of the pool, they started with a great splash and then settled into long steady strokes.

She beat him on the first lap, but she was straining and Alex seemed to be cutting along without the least effort. By the second lap he'd taken a slight lead.

His long arms and legs chopped up the water while she ploughed through it arduously. Finally Patti relaxed and let herself admire the smooth athletic workings of his body as he surged forward to win by half a length.

"I should have bet on that race," Alex said as they leaned against the side of the pool in the shallow end. "I could have made you cook dinner."

"You could do that anyway," she reminded him. "If you don't mind frozen food."

"You don't cook?"

"Well, actually, yes, but I tend to throw in whatever's at hand. How are you on lima bean, tuna fish, and left-over macaroni 'n' cheese casseroles?"

"Sounds disgusting." He hoisted himself up on his forearms and jackknifed out of the pool.

"Show-off," Patti said as she sloshed up the concrete steps.

He grinned and held out a towel. When she tried to take it, he pulled it back with a shake of the head and then rubbed it slowly to and fro across her arms and back.

The rough feel of the terry exhilarated her skin. This could be dangerous, Patti thought.

"Enough!" She snatched the towel away. "Go dry yourself before you catch pneumonia."

"It's nearly ninety degrees out today," he responded. "Speaking of which, I'm thirsty. And hungry. How about a snack?"

They wandered into the kitchen together. "Do you have any potato chips?" Patti asked.

"I beg your pardon?"

"Well, you mentioned a snack."

"I didn't say anything about poisoning yourself with junk food," Alex replied. "Have a seat."

She perched on one of the kitchen chairs while he removed a butter dish, a brie cheese, and a small jar of sliced almonds from the refrigerator.

Carefully, he cut off a chunk of butter and dropped it into a copper pan along with a handful of almonds, then put away the butter dish and the jar. Peeling the paper cover from the brie, he set it in the pan and covered it.

"That looks like a lot of work," she said.

"It just takes a minute." He ruffled the towel through his hair.

"I've never understood why men bother with hair-dryers," Patti observed. "Your hair is so short it must dry in five minutes anyway."

"You're reasonably short yourself, but that doesn't mean you're easy to manage," he fired back, producing a package of wheat crackers from the pantry and setting them out on a stoneware plate. "Sure, it'll dry by itself, if I don't mind looking like Harpo Marx."

It was harder than ever to reconcile this virile, teasing male with the starchily proper Vice Mayor Greene she'd met at City Hall.

"The brie should be heated through by now." Still drying his hair with one hand, he reached for the pan.

"Ow!" He pulled back sharply.

Patti jumped up. "Did you burn yourself?"

"That's what I get for not paying attention," he muttered, cradling his injured hand as she switched off the burner and moved the pan to the back of the stove.

"Let me look at it. I studied first aid, along with cardiopulmonary resuscitation and a few other things that come in handy with senior citizens." Patti took his hand in hers, inspecting the skin that was already beginning to blister.

"I seem to recall hearing that you're supposed to put butter on a burn," Alex said.

"Absolutely not!" She led him over to the sink and carefully washed his hand with cold water. "That's the worst thing you can do."

"What's the best thing?"

"Ice," she said. "Hold on." Moving quickly, Patti fetched a washcloth from the bathroom and wrapped it around an ice cube to make an impromptu cold pack. "Hold this on the burn. It'll numb the pain and start the healing process. If you like, we can drop by the drugstore and pick up some ointment, but it doesn't look serious."

"Thanks. It's nice to have someone around who knows what she's doing."

Patti shrugged off the compliment. "Oh, I can do a few things right. Shall I serve the brie?"

"Please do." He sat at the table and watched as she

flipped the brie onto the plate so the almonds were on top. "I have a feeling you'd be an excellent cook if you wanted to."

The cheese was heated through, rich and creamy. Patti took a bite and let the flavor percolate through her taste buds. "That's delicious. I can't believe it was that easy to fix."

She sat beside him, helping scoop up some cheese on a cracker for him. Finally he laid the ice pack aside.

"It's not hurting anymore. Thanks to you." His uninjured hand alighted on her bare shoulders, playing softly across the delicate bones.

Absentmindedly she took another bite of the cheese as he intensified his sensual sonata.

"It's strange how you seem to belong here," Alex murmured. "As if this house were designed with you in mind."

Startled, she looked to see if he was joking, but his expression was serious. "How can you say that? I mean, it's beautiful, but it isn't my kind of house at all."

"Isn't it?" he said.

"Well . . . I mean . . ." I mean it's too perfect, too stifling! she thought. And yet another part of her found the place comfortable and welcoming.

"You have an innate elegance, even though you're fighting it," he said.

Alex reached out and caught her wrist, drawing her onto his lap. Taken by surprise, she yielded, and at once became intensely aware of his body pressed close to hers.

Strong, gentle hands cupped her face and he searched her eyes before bringing his mouth down onto hers. His kiss was different from before, no longer probing but confident.

Patti anchored herself to his powerful forearms. His tongue commanded and hers obeyed. She was made of steamy water, without a will except to part beneath the swimmer's dive.

Alex traced the expanse of her cheekbones, the throb

of her temples, the dainty shell of her ears. Fingertips whispered in a wordless language that she understood instinctively.

They did fit together in so many ways, she realized. It would be so easy to lose herself in him, to live the sort of life she'd been raised to accept.

Every sense responded to him. She smelled his musky desire, heard the way his breath came harshly. And now she was tasting him again, lips against lips, hungry and prowling.

She had to stop before they went too far. If she let this man take her, he would take her emotions as well. There was nothing fly-by-night about Alex Greene. Quite the contrary. He was stable, respectable, distinguished.

The kind of man who would tuck her neatly into his exquisite home and his prepackaged life. She would never be seen again except smiling politely at business associates, making small talk while she wore the right clothes to blandly forgettable parties.

Why did he have to be this way? she wondered, agonized. He'd made it all too clear earlier what his idea of a wife was—someone who dabbled with watercolors, as long as it didn't interfere with anything really important, like keeping the house clean.

"Alex." It hurt her to stop him, and yet she must. "Please. I want to get up."

He relinquished her reluctantly, his hands lingering on her arms as she eased back into her own seat.

"Patti, I'm willing to take this slowly," Alex said, leaning forward and meeting her gaze directly. "I know you've been hurt before, and you have to learn to trust me."

"It's not a question of trust." She shivered, beginning to feel cold with only the skimpy bathing suit to protect her from the air-conditioned coolness.

"Yes, it is. You have to learn to trust that I really care about you—about Patti Lyon, a very capable and intelligent and lovely young woman," Alex said.

"Alex, we're wrong for each other." It hurt to say it, but she had to.

"You haven't given us a chance," he countered. "You formed a snap judgment based on one aspect of my life, my position on the city council and my opposition to poker parlors. There's a lot more to me than that."

"I know there is," Patti said. "I saw how you have concern for people, how you care about the Nunezes. I know your feelings about gambling aren't based on selfish concerns. But the way you live and the way I live—just aren't compatible."

"I hardly think that whether I drop my clothes on the floor or not is going to make any significant difference." Alex's tone lightened, as if he'd already won the battle.

"It isn't that!" Patti struggled to find the right words. "But everything's so cut and dried in your life. I can't imagine you, say, going on a game show, the way I do."

"Oh, I don't know," Alex said, leaning back in his chair. "I've always thought that would be fun."

"You have not."

"I've even watched game shows a couple of times." He grinned. "Although I missed the ones you were on. My misfortune."

The man knew how to play poker, Patti thought. She had the feeling he was bluffing now, and doing it expertly, but she was going to call him on it.

"Well, you may get your chance," she said. "They're starting a spin-off of *Lady Luck* that uses couples. We may be able to try out in a week or so, if you're serious about this."

"Sure." He didn't bat an eye. "Let me know when you have the details."

As if to demonstrate how easy he was to get along with, Alex spent the rest of the evening challenging her to a series of board games—he won Monopoly, she won Trivial Pursuit—and sharing take-out Chinese food.

"I apologize for the modest repast," he teased. "If I weren't an invalid, it would be dinner and dancing."

His hand had blistered a little, but otherwise looked all right, Patti noted with relief, examining it as they sat at the kitchen table finishing up their moo shu pork. "Be sure to keep that clean," she said, and then smiled devilishly. "As if you ever got anything dirty..."

"Not if I can help it," he agreed. "And now I'm afraid my eight hours are up."

How typical of him to be watching the clock! Patti seized on this new criticism eagerly, convincing herself—or trying to—that the man was indeed an impossible case.

They drove back to her house in companionable silence. At her front door, Alex grazed her lips with his own in a perfectly proper good-night kiss. Just as she'd expected. And yet... the feelings that proper kiss had aroused were not proper at all.

"I'll pick you up next Saturday. Ten A.M."

She nodded, suddenly unable to speak, and watched him return to the dark-red Mustang before letting herself into the house.

For one blinding instant she yearned to run outside and summon him back, into her arms and into her heart. It was with mingled relief and sadness that she heard the car pull away.

There were so many things about him that attracted her, but she mustn't give in. He was too much like Mark.

She'd almost forgotten it, but she and Mark had enjoyed some good times together during their courtship—a trip to Hearst Castle, a tour of the wine country. But once they'd settled down to real life, everything had changed.

She wouldn't make the same mistake again.

- 4 -

PATTI FELT OUT of sync for the next few days, bouncing around her exercise classes and chatting with her elderly students as if nothing had changed from the week before.

Things certainly had changed, at least in the landscape of her mind. At the oddest moments memories of Alex jutted up like mountains in a mist.

She pictured him sitting in his den, listening intently, drawing her out with questions. Or talking to Sister Anna, his forehead creased with concern as he glanced at Rosa Nunez.

He was a man who cared a great deal about others. Serving on the city council, she knew from talking to Irene, was an unpaid position that involved a lot of work.

And most of all, she liked him. He possessed a zest for life that was rare in men she'd known, and strangely at odds with the image Alex had projected the first time they met. She sensed there was more to him than one might guess.

Her common sense warned her to beware, but Patti

wasn't in the habit of playing it safe.

Besides, she told herself, surely there could be no harm in a mild flirtation with Alex. They enjoyed each other's company, and he said himself that he hadn't yet found the woman he wanted to settle down with.

Settle down! Patti smiled to herself as she slipped into a pair of plum-colored slacks on Saturday morning. Even someone as sure of himself as Alex couldn't help figuring out sooner or later that she wasn't the domestic type.

She completed her outfit with a pink sweater that flattered her dark hair and eyes. Heaven knew where they'd end up today; she hoped her outfit wouldn't look out of place.

In the middle of drawing a brush through her hair, Patti stared at herself in the mirror with astonishment.

What on earth was she thinking? Hoping that her outfit wouldn't look out of place!

"Next thing you know, I'll be flinging the word *appropriate* around," she muttered in disgust.

The doorbell rang. What timing! Patti had to force a smile as she went to greet Alex.

She forgot her annoyance as soon as she opened the door and saw the warmth shining in his eyes.

He was dressed more casually than usual, in tailored tan slacks and a heather-green cashmere sweater that made him look young and touchable.

Every fiber of her being responded instinctively to the strong male body standing only two feet away, and her mouth could already taste the kiss even before he brushed it across her lips.

"Good morning, beautiful," Alex murmured. "I was half afraid my sprite would have vanished during the week."

Did that mean he'd missed her? Patti warmed to his endearments. Beautiful. Sprite. Unbidden, an answer came to mind, trembling on her tongue—I've missed you, too. She couldn't allow herself to speak the words. But oh, they were there.

"How's your hand?" she asked.

"It's made a full recovery." He showed her where pink new skin had grown over the burn. They leaned together, and the contact proved more than Patti could resist.

Her arms circled his neck and he pulled her against him. Gentle hands stroked her hair, which she'd left loose and flowing. Alex's nose tickled her cheek and ear, and she realized he was inhaling her fragrance just as she was reveling in his musk scent.

Then, to her disappointment, he drew away. "I'm afraid you'll have to give me a rain check. We've got a commitment—unfortunately."

Patti leaned against the door frame. "Don't you ever just let life flow along?"

He ruffled her hair where it lay along one shoulder, stirring darts of fire beneath his touch. "That does sound like a lovely idea. As a matter of fact, that's exactly what I have in mind for this afternoon."

Shaking her head, Patti said, "You've got it all wrong. You can't schedule it . . . That's like saying, 'Hey, let's plan to be spontaneous at two o'clock!'"

A chuckle greeted her remark. "Touché," Alex said. "If there weren't other people involved, I'd sweep you off into the noonday sun, but . . ."

He shrugged, and Patti knew better than to argue further. There was no use fighting it. Alex might indeed let himself get carried away by passion from time to time, but only if it fitted into his agenda.

Their destination turned out to be the remodeled house where the Help Center was to be established. The property was already being used by counselors for a drug diversion program funded by the city.

The white stucco house was about sixty years old—ancient for Citrus Grove—and designed with a Spanish flavor. It had a large front porch and an arching front door, which contributed to the homey, old-fashioned effect.

Inside, the living room and bedrooms had been redone to create an environment that bridged the gap between an office and a house—just right for a community service center, Patti thought, appreciating the mellow ochre paint on the walls and the newly installed champagne carpeting.

"They're really doing a good job here," she said. "Some of the council members are on the board of directors, aren't they?"

Before Alex could answer, a bearded young man wearing wire-rimmed glasses emerged from the hallway and came to greet them.

Alex made the introductions. Frank Straub was head of the drug diversion program and filling in as temporary director of the Help Center until other groups moved into the house.

"I'm really eager to get back to counseling full time," he explained to Patti as they settled onto a sofa in what had once been the living room. "But somebody had to keep things rolling until the center's ready to hire a full-time director."

"Sister Anna's program will be headquartered here during the week, although they'll continue to use the church auditorium for Sunday distribution," Alex noted, and Patti nodded appreciatively.

"Have you heard anything more about Rosa Nunez?" she asked. "Sister Anna seemed worried about her."

Instead of Alex, it was Frank who spoke up. "I know the fellow she's been dating—Jim Arruga. Maybe he'll get himself straightened out one of these days—I certainly hope so—but right now he's bad news."

Patti wished she could think of something brilliant to do to help with Rosa. "Do you suppose I could talk to her . . ."

Before she could finish, the exterior door opened and four men came in. One, judging by his casual hairstyle and clothing was also a drug counselor. The other three had neatly clipped hair and trim mustaches.

Policemen, Patti thought instinctively, and it turned out she was right.

The officers and counselors had requested the meeting, Alex explained, to air their concerns about the poker parlor proposal.

"Since you're one of the key advocates, I thought it only fair that you be present," he said, and the other men nodded, taking the statement at face value.

Patti's lips tightened. How typical of a corporation president to buy himself a female "slave" and then spend the time trying to win her support on a political issue!

Had she misjudged Alex in other ways, too? She couldn't figure out how a man could be overwhelmingly romantic one minute and as prosaic as a clod of dirt the next.

She felt somewhat at a loss as the men began talking. After all, they were experts in their fields, and she was just an exercise instructor who liked to try out for game shows.

But quickly she forgot her reservations, getting absorbed in what was being said.

The officers and the counselors alike were concerned primarily with the possibility of organized crime moving into the area.

"The Mafia has had a hard time getting established in southern California because our population is so spread out and diverse," explained a sergeant who served as public liaison for the police department.

The other two officers, she'd learned, were vice and narcotics detectives.

"This might give them a toehold," agreed Frank Straub. "I'm especially concerned because organized crime is heavily involved in drugs."

Patti listened thoughtfully to the various concerns. Certainly these men dealt with an aspect of life in Citrus Grove that she had never encountered.

Still, she felt entitled to her opinion, and finally she stated it.

"I'm not an expert, and I'd be strongly opposed to poker if it meant the mob would move in," she said. "But isn't it also possible that a legalized, regulated betting operation would undercut any attempts at illicit gambling?"

The men conceded that she had a point.

"The key, I think, is regulation," admitted the sergeant. "How do we make sure the management is clean?"

The meeting went on for another quarter of an hour. The sergeant agreed to check with police in communities that had such parlors and find out what their experiences had been.

"I guess I wasn't much help," Patti said as she and Alex emerged into the sunlight. "But I do think people are overreacting."

"We'll find out when we learn what's happened in other towns." Alex laid his arm possessively around her waist. "Now, why don't we go do something spontaneous for a couple of hours?"

She had to laugh. "I'll leave it to you."

"Well, in that case..."

Half an hour later, Alex's Mustang pulled into a newly vacated parking space in the Lido Village shopping area. The "village" bordered an inlet of Newport Harbor, and Patti breathed in the tangy sea air with pleasure.

"I haven't been down here in months," she said.

"Good. Then you won't mind staying for lunch." Alex held the car door open while she slid out.

"More take-out chicken?" she teased.

"Oh, well, if that's what you want..." He started back toward the driver's side.

"No! A joke! Honest!"

He grinned and linked his arm through hers. "Glad to hear it."

They walked along the waterfront, window-shopping in the boutiques to their right and, alternately, gazing at the sailboats bobbing in the water to their left.

Before long, they came to a shop that featured espresso coffee and sandwiches on whole-wheat bread. Patti selected a tuna melt and Alex went for pastrami, which they ate sitting outside at a round ice-cream table.

The sea air soothed them, rich with the scent of brine and hinting at mermaids and lost galleons. Patti felt as if they'd traveled very far from Citrus Grove into some exotic other world.

"When I was a kid in Boston, I used to dream about running away to sea," Alex mused, staring over the water. Across from them, two young men were untethering a boat with bright multicolored sails.

"Somehow I can't see you swabbing the decks and getting tattooed with naked ladies," Patti admitted.

Alex's chuckle was dryly ironic. "Oh, it was just that sometimes I felt a little confined."

"Why didn't you take up watercolors?" Patti asked, and held her breath, wondering if he'd be offended.

"Watercolors?" He looked puzzled.

"Like your mother." She tried to explain. "That was meant as a joke—well, a half-serious one. You seemed to think that her dabbling in watercolors was as wild and creative an act as anyone could wish for."

"Did I say that?" Alex chuckled. "How pompous of me."

Refreshed by his candor, Patti laughed, too. "Anyway, tell me why you felt confined."

Alex sipped thoughtfully at his cappuccino. "I really like my family. My dad's an engineer and my mother, as you know, likes to paint. My older brother's an engineer, too; he and Dad are partners in the firm Dad started."

A tugboat chugged along the channel in front of them, and Alex paused to watch.

"That sounds almost a little bit too cozy," Patti said.

He nodded. "I'd always been interested in engineering myself, but I couldn't see myself fitting quietly into the background—the younger brother, a junior member of the firm. And Boston began to feel confining, too, although it's a fascinating city. The problem was that I'd grown up there and all my friends knew each other and everything began to seem too predictable."

"So you came west?" she asked. "Seeking your fortune?"

"In a manner of speaking," Alex agreed. "As a matter of fact, you're likely to learn more about that than you really want to know, in a few minutes. Finished with your lunch?"

"Yes. What—"

"You'll see." He disposed of their trash and they returned to the car.

Patti glanced at her watch. "Gosh, it's only half past noon. It feels like we've done a lot today."

He agreed, then added, "Say, if you like to act on the spur of the moment, how come you wear a watch?"

She leaned against the cushy seat as Alex backed up and headed out of the parking lot. "I have to or I'd be late for all my classes. So now I put it on every morning out of habit. What's your excuse?"

"I like wearing a watch," he said.

She examined his digital model. It looked as if it contained everything but a calculator, and she wouldn't have wanted to bet it didn't have one of those, too.

Beneath the watch his wrist was strong and supple. Patti's attention drifted to the masterful way he gripped the steering wheel, swinging them across the bridge that led to Lido Island.

He could do a lot of things with those hands. Wonderful things, she had reason to believe.

Maybe he was thinking the same thing, because his breath came faster and when he paused at a stop sign, his eyes sought Patti's.

His gaze locked her in place with its penetrating intensity. Without thinking, she licked her lips nervously, and noted with a shock of passion how his own tongue passed lightly over his upper lip, as if inviting her inside.

A car honked behind them.

"Patience, patience," Alex muttered, and turned to the left.

The streets of Lido Isle were lined with houses pressed tightly together. Many presented a blank wall to passersby, which meant that the rooms probably focused inward, on a central courtyard. But despite the high density, Patti knew even a modest residence here could cost a quarter of a million dollars.

The reason was obvious. The island was right in the middle of one of the loveliest small-boat harbors in the world. The houses located around the rim of Lido even had their own boat slips—a priceless treasure, considering that there was a years-long waiting list for public moorings.

Alex found a parking space along the street and backed carefully into it.

"Nicely done," Patti said. "I usually have to hike to the curb when I parallel park."

"Get a lot of tickets?"

"Mostly hate mail from other drivers." She popped out of the car. "It's not that I don't try to do a good job. I can't figure out what the problem is."

"Fear of precision," Alex observed knowingly.

He did have a point, she admitted silently as he caught her hand and pulled her across the street.

They passed through a decorative grillwork gate into a small yard that was really more of a patio, with huge pots of geraniums surrounding an outdoor table and chairs.

"Who are we visiting?" Patti asked.

Alex rang the doorbell. "My former partner."

The door opened a crack and an apron-clad, middle-aged woman peered out. "Yes? Oh, Mr. Greene!"

The woman opened the door and ushered them inside. "I'll tell Mr. and Mrs. Burke you're here."

A housekeeper and everything, Patti thought as they walked from the entrance hall into a vast living room with a splendid view of the harbor through a wall of glass.

The furniture consisted of dark, finely wrought antiques set against an ivory carpet. The paintings on the walls were all originals by famous Impressionists.

"Alex!" A large man strode into the room, crossing to clap Alex on the back. "Glad you could drop by!"

"Ed, this is my friend Patti Lyon," Alex said, and Patti found her hand clasped in Ed's giant one.

"Glad to meet you, little lady," he boomed. "And this is my wife, Marion."

Marion had slipped into the room so quietly Patti hadn't even realized she was there. A sweet-faced woman with a shy smile, she merely nodded at Patti without speaking.

The housekeeper returned with a coffeepot, cups, and a plate of crisp, honey-flavored cookies. She left the tray on the table and Marion began serving everyone.

"Please have a seat," Ed said. "We were hoping Alex would bring you by to show you the boat today, like he said he might." He waved out the window at a small private dock, at which a sleek sailboat bobbed invitingly. "We're still partners in the *Optical Illusion*"—which, Patti gathered, was the name of the boat—"even though I sold him my half of Greene Optics. Used to be Greene-Burke Optics, but it's gotten a lot bigger since then."

He shot a fond, almost fatherly look at Alex.

"I'm afraid I don't know a whole lot about Greene Optics," Patti said.

"One of these days I'll give you the grand tour," Alex

offered. "We make everything from lenses to holograms."

"Management was my specialty, but Alex has gotten really good at that," Ed went on. "His strength, though, was innovation. He's always looking ahead."

"Well, I came along at the right time." Alex's eyes sparkled with excitement. "Lasers offer an incredible range of possibilities."

"Now, now, we wouldn't want to bore the ladies with technical talk," Ed commented with a wink at Patti.

She wanted to protest that she wouldn't be bored at all. As a matter of fact, she couldn't help resenting Ed's patronizing attitude, yet she realized that he meant no harm.

"How about you?" she asked Marion, who was perched on a tapestried antique chair. "What are you interested in?"

"Oh, I just look after Ed." Marion gazed adoringly at her husband.

They finished their coffee and cookies, making polite conversation about Lido Isle and the weather.

"There's a storm coming up, according to the weather report," Ed remarked. "You aren't planning to take 'er out today, are you, Alex?"

Patti turned toward the window. The sailboat danced beside the pier like a spirited horse champing at the bit. "I'd love to go sailing," she said wistfully.

"I suppose a turn around the harbor wouldn't hurt," Alex said, smiling at her fondly.

The Burkes walked them down to the pier and watched while Alex rigged the sails, explaining as he did so that the *Optical Illusion* was a type of sailboat called a sloop. Patti tried to look knowledgeable, although in fact she'd never been sailing in a small boat before.

"Here you go." Alex handed her a life jacket.

"I can swim," Patti said.

"Doesn't pay to take chances, little lady," Ed commented. "You should be safe enough in the harbor, but you never can tell. Especially with a storm coming up. Well, we'll leave you young folks alone. Be careful! Pleasure to meet you, Miss Lyon."

Marion smiled her farewell, and the couple strolled back up to their house.

"Does Marion always chatter away like that?" Patti asked.

"What?" Occupied by rigging the sail, Alex took a minute to realize she was kidding. "Oh, she's the quiet type. Makes a good match with Ed."

Marion certainly looked happy, Patti reflected. Patti almost wished she herself had that kind of take-a-backseat personality. It would certainly have made her life a lot easier. But duller, she reminded herself.

Alex cast off, enlisting Patti's help in releasing the lines. She tried to watch closely how he handled the sails, but after nearly getting swept overboard by the boom, she decided to pay more attention to her own end of the boat.

"From time to time we talk about getting a yacht, but this is more fun," Alex called as he guided them away from the dock.

The air was cold and brisk over the water, and tangy with saltwater spray. Patti felt exhilarated as they swung toward the main channel.

Everything looked different from this perspective. The houses on both sides of the harbor turned their true faces toward the water, with broad windows and flower-filled terraces.

"This is fun!" she called as they rolled over a slight swell.

"It's my escape," Alex admitted. "My family used to sail at Cape Cod in the summer."

Patti waved at a teenager who sailed by in a tiny catboat not much bigger than a bathtub. The boy waved back and took a swig from a can of beer.

"That's dangerous," Alex noted. "Drinking and sailing can be deadly. People don't realize that the sea is nothing to fool around with. Even inside the harbor, you can drown."

"Cheerful thought." Patti wished he wouldn't always take life so seriously. The point of sailing was to have fun, wasn't it? "Can't we go outside the harbor? It doesn't look like bad weather to me."

There were a few dark clouds to the north, but otherwise no sign of the promised storm. The clouds might easily pass by without any problem, she thought. October marked the start of southern California's rainy season, but the weather was mostly sunny and placid. And weather forecasts were often wrong.

"We can go near the jetties, anyway," Alex conceded. "I hope you didn't mind my taking you to meet the Burkes. Ed means a lot to me. He's been kind of a second father."

"So I gathered." Patti felt a twinge of envy. She'd longed to be close to her own father, but he held up such high standards. And unfortunately, his standards were often different from hers.

As Alex eased the sailboat along, Patti rested her head on his shoulder. It was peaceful out here, with only the soft whisper of waves against the boat and the catlike cry of sea gulls overhead.

Instinctively, Patti huddled closer to Alex to keep warm, and he tipped up her chin, his mouth coming down to meet hers.

His lips were cold on the outside but oh so warm within as they kissed, slowly and tenderly. Patti could taste the salt spray on his skin and feel the trace of wetness as she ruffled her fingers through his hair.

Their caresses took on a timeless quality, as if the two of them were floating in space. Slowly they tasted each other, explored crevices and hollows, the damp heat left by his tongue quickly whipped away in the cool air.

Finally he released her. "I'd better pay attention before I run this boat into a dock," Alex said ruefully.

The wind had picked up as they approached the harbor entrance, and Patti was grateful for the warmth of the life vest. She'd forgotten that even on a warm day the air could be chilly over water; that must be why there weren't many boats out sailing today.

Beyond the jetties the sea swelled and subsided. The sight of open ocean proved unexpectedly thrilling. Patti felt like an explorer, on the rim of vast new territory.

Alex began to bring the boat around.

"Can't we go just a little farther?" Patti asked. "It doesn't seem as if we've really been sailing, not even leaving the harbor."

"Well." He brushed some salt spray from his eyes. "It's probably not a good idea."

Patti believed in safety, but he was being overcautious. "Can't we just take a quick swing into the ocean? It feels so free and wild, zipping along with the sails flapping."

After a moment's consideration he gave in. "Okay. I don't suppose it will hurt."

She grinned in anticipation. "Thanks."

There was, as she had expected, a sharp delight in escaping the boundaries of the harbor. For a delicious moment Patti felt as if they were suspended between sea and sky and might take off in flight at any moment.

Then a wave lifted the boat just as a sharp gust of wind caught the sails and tilted them sharply.

"Damn!" Alex hurriedly lowered the mainsail. Patti's efforts to help only seemed to get in the way, so she finally sat on one of the benches and remained silent as she attempted to balance herself against the thrust of the now-choppy sea.

It couldn't have been more than ten agonizing minutes of fighting the wind before Alex brought them back into the calm of the harbor, but to Patti it felt like hours.

He glared as he piloted their way back between rows

of moored boats. "We could have been in real trouble out there. That storm must be coming in."

"I'm sorry," Patti said.

"No, it's my fault. I should have known better." He sounded angry.

They arrived at the dock in a silence broken only by Alex's terse instructions on tying up the boat. A lump formed in Patti's chest.

Regardless of what Alex said, it was she who'd put them in danger, she who'd kept pushing him to sail outside the harbor. She hadn't believed it could really be dangerous, and besides, the ocean looked so alluring.

They stowed away their life jackets and climbed up the steps from the dock.

Her legs felt wobbly on land, already missing the easy sway of the boat. Patti wanted to ask if they could go sailing again some other time, but she didn't dare.

He had every right to be angry at her, Patti thought as they returned to the car. She was glad the Burkes didn't make a repeat appearance; right now, she wasn't in the mood to be sociable.

On the drive home Alex kept his attention focused on the road. "I can't believe I was such a damn fool," he said. "And with a storm warning out, too."

Such a damn fool to listen to me, Patti thought unhappily.

She'd taken a few risks over the years—once she'd even tried parachuting, which had proved exciting but also terrifying. However, she'd rarely done anything so careless as to endanger another person. The lure of the ocean had been strong—stronger than her judgment, she realized.

Alex pulled up in front of her house and walked her to the door. "I apologize for nearly drowning both of us," he said.

"It wasn't your fault. It was mine." Patti wished she could erase that grim look from his face.

He turned and walked away without even answering.

Patti entered and leaned against the inside of the door for several minutes, half hoping he would come back, until finally she heard the car move away.

Well, Patti thought unhappily, that's the end of that. And it's all my fault.

She changed into old clothes and began furiously vacuuming the rug.

- 5 -

THE TELEPHONE RANG about noon on Monday, while Patti was home for lunch between exercise classes.

Her heart catapulted into her throat. She hadn't heard from Alex since their near disaster on Saturday. If he was still angry about the incident, she couldn't blame him.

She picked up the receiver. "Hello?"

"Miss Lyon?" A male voice, but definitely not Alex's.

Trying not to sound disappointed, she said, "Yes?"

"This is Bill from *Double Luck*. We wondered if you and your partner could come down tomorrow to audition. I realize this is kind of short notice, but we just got the go-ahead and we're on a tight schedule."

"Oh, sure," she responded automatically, jotting down the time. The address was the same as before.

It wasn't until after he clicked off that she remembered that she didn't have a partner lined up yet. At least not officially.

Patti hesitated, her hand resting atop the telephone.

Alex had said he was interested, back when. Did she dare call him now?

She certainly couldn't handle much more of this uncertainty, she decided. If he didn't want to see her again, she'd rather find out about it sooner than later.

After flipping through the phone book, she found the number for Greene Optics and placed the call. The switchboard operator put her through to a very efficient-sounding secretary.

"Mr. Greene, please," Patti said. "This is Miss Lyon calling."

"Does he know what this is in reference to?" asked the clipped female voice.

"Yes." Patti hoped the woman wouldn't press her further. She felt relieved when she was put on hold.

"Patti?" Alex sounded so warm and pleased that she wanted to hug him over the phone line.

"I'm sorry to bother you at work," she began.

"That's all right. Is anything wrong?"

"No." The tension seeped out of her body. He wasn't mad at her anymore, then. "I got a call from the producer of that new game show I was telling you about."

She filled him in on the details. "Are you interested?"

"Tomorrow at ten?" She could hear him flipping through the pages of a desk calendar. "Yes, I can get away. Shall I pick you up at nine?"

"Yes, fine." Dazedly, she said good-bye and rang off.

The rest of the day and evening crept by with maddening slowness, and Patti slept restlessly, awakening early.

She changed her clothes three times, finally settled on a pink linen shirtdress, and was ready half an hour early.

"You look terrific," Alex said warmly when he arrived. "None the worse for our near-shipwreck?"

"No, I'm fine." She cuddled against him for a moment at the door, and then they walked to the car together.

"Alex, I'm really sorry. I should never have pushed you to leave the harbor."

"It's not your fault, it's mine," he responded, his expression sobering. "You can't be expected to know how dangerous the sea can be, but I'm an experienced sailor."

Patti decided to drop the subject. Instead, as they drove she refreshed him on the rules of the *Luck* game.

It was based on a combination of poker and trivia. First each couple was given a poker "hand" generated by a computer—instead of actual cards, the faces were shown on an electronic scoreboard in front of the contestants. As in poker, there were five "cards," and one was to try and make poker hands, such as flushes and straights.

As in poker, contestants had to decide what to discard, up to a maximum of three cards. But in order to win a chance at drawing replacements, they first had to answer trivia questions.

"So there's both skill and luck involved," Alex observed. "It's a good game—I'm looking forward to this."

"You didn't just come because I talked you into it?" Patti asked.

"I'll admit I'd never have considered doing it on my own." He glanced over at her with a smile. "You see, you're opening up new horizons for me."

She couldn't tell whether he was kidding.

They arrived in Hollywood with plenty of time to spare. Inside the audition room with about two dozen other couples, Patti nodded to some of the people she recognized from the previous audition.

Alex studied the scene with interest. "I'd expected a TV studio or something. This looks like a classroom."

"They do tape in a studio, I'm sure," Patti said. "This is behind the scenes. It's never as glamorous as it looks from out front."

"There may be a universal truth in there, but I'm not

in the mood to be profound," Alex said.

Soon Bill arrived and began the game. Patti found that she and Alex worked well together with a natural understanding that made them a formidable team.

"Too bad we're not playing for real," Alex murmured as they won their round.

Afterward, Bill read off a list of names. Patti's and Alex's were on it.

"I'd like for these couples to stay after the rest of you leave. Thanks for coming, everyone," he said.

About half the couples left, calling out "Good luck!" to those who remained.

"They're certainly good sports about losing," Alex said.

"They can always come and try out again," Patti said. "But I've noticed that most people seem to realize they're competing against themselves more than each other."

Bill's announcement cut her short. "Well, ladies and gentlemen, congratulations. We'd like you to join us for *Double Luck.*" There was a smattering of applause. "That's the good news. The not-so-great news is that we start taping at noon on Friday, which I realize is short notice. How many of you can make it then?"

Patti shot Alex a questioning look. He took out a small calendar and consulted it.

"There's a League of Cities meeting at nine A.M. in Los Angeles," he murmured. "I'd have to meet you at the studio. Is that all right?"

"Sure," she said.

As they signed up she noticed Alex frowning. Was he sorry he'd gotten involved?

"You can back out if you want to," she said.

"No. I just hope the meeting doesn't run over." He bent to write his name and phone number on the list.

They drove down Sunset Boulevard to the Beverly Hills Hotel, where they ate lunch at the Polo Lounge, seafood salads for both of them, and then drove back to Citrus Grove.

"I'm afraid I'm tied up for the rest of the week," Alex said as he dropped her off at home. "So I'll see you Friday at the studio."

"Great." Patti leaned over to kiss him, her nerves tingling at the touch of his lips.

His hand cupped the back of her head for a moment and their eyes met. After a moment he released her.

Patti climbed slowly out of the car. That brief glance into the depths of each other's eyes had felt more intimate than any embrace.

She was going to have to watch herself. It would be so easy to get lost in her feelings for Alex, to forget temporarily about her own needs, to give in to anything he asked.

Auditioning together had been exhilarating—but she and Alex were basically different, Patti reminded herself. Very, very different.

Her doubts returned. Would he really show up for *Double Luck* and risk making a fool of himself on nationwide television? Game shows might be lighthearted entertainment, but you could look awfully stupid if you botched things. And he had the perfect excuse not to be there—the League of Cities meeting.

"Why would he try out if he wasn't interested?" Irene asked Wednesday evening as they sat sipping coffee in the Ramirezes' kitchen.

"Maybe he was interested, but he's having second thoughts." Patti brushed a wisp of hair back to anchor it behind her ears.

"You worry too much," said Irene.

"But when you think about it, why should he bother? He doesn't need the money," Patti said. "And suppose we're a big flop?"

Irene shrugged. "I can't imagine Alex Greene getting

upset about a little thing like that."

Patti tried to pin down what was bothering her. "It's just not in keeping with his character. Everything in his life seems so tidy and precise. I can't picture him going on national television, in front of millions of people, playing a card game—why, he doesn't even believe in legalized gambling!"

"But you're not really gambling," Irene pointed out. "If you lose, you don't really lose anything."

"Well, let's hope he thinks about it that way," Patti said.

On Friday she found herself wishing Alex were driving into the city with her. An attack of nerves—an experience she'd had before every game show appearance—made her hands feel slippery on the steering wheel as she drove to the studio in Burbank. And the gray overcast sky didn't improve her spirits any.

Patti had brought two changes of clothing, as the show's organizers requested. It was a standard procedure on game shows. Couples on *Double Luck* could appear on up to three shows, which would air on consecutive days, and it would look strange if a woman wore the same dress for three days in a row.

At the studio's performers' entrance, a woman with a clipboard checked off Patti's name. "What about Alex Greene?" she asked, reading from her list.

"He's coming separately," Patti explained, and was directed back to the makeup room.

After having her skin coated into plastic perfection, Patti joined the other contestants in a dressing room. She found two vacant folding chairs and took one, noticing how everyone else sat in couples.

They were taping three shows today, she recalled, with two couples competing on each. A total of seven pairs had been invited, just in case someone had to cancel—which was beginning to look like a strong possibility, in her case.

Gossip ran rife, as it usually did among high-strung competitors backstage.

"I hear the top-dollar prize is double that on *Lady Luck,*" said a short, round-faced man wearing a plaid suit. "Thirty-five thousand smackeroos! Wowee."

"Jerry's great at this sort of thing," his wife said to no one in particular. She was a tall woman with a ramrod straight spine and short, silvered hair.

"Oh, boy, you guys better watch out when I get my turn!" Jerry whooped.

A young couple across from Patti smiled at each other, sharing their amusement. It made her miss Alex even more.

She should never have talked him into coming, Patti told herself. He'd probably only agreed because, when they first discussed it, she'd practically dared him.

It was five minutes to twelve, and Bill walked in, nodding to everyone. He drew out a list and began calling off names. Patti swallowed hard. This was going to be embarrassing.

"Alex Greene?" Bill said at last.

"Here." The deep voice from the doorway drew everyone's attention.

Alex filled up the door frame, a light-gray suit emphasizing the breadth of his shoulders. Patti found herself grinning at him, then quickly looked away.

"Sorry. There was a wreck on the freeway and I got held up," he muttered as he slid into the folding chair beside her.

"Oh, that's okay," Patti said with as much nonchalance as she could muster.

With everyone accounted for, Bill marched them into the studio and they took turns standing behind a counter and speaking into tiny microphones clipped to their lapels.

"Hi, everybody!" It was Argo Galoof, a stand-up comic who'd been selected as the show's emcee. He was a beanpole of a man with fake buck teeth and a mop of hair that she was sure must be a wig. Patti had seen him on several television variety shows and found him a bit corny for her taste. "How's everybody doing?"

"Hi, yourself!" It was the plaid-suited contestant named Jerry. "Glad to be on board!"

At this bold response Argo Galoof's nostrils flared as if he'd smelled a bad odor, but he quickly recovered and gave them all a beatific smile.

"Looks like he's going to get some competition from one of the contestants," Alex said in a low voice as they filed into tiered seats to one side of the small audience.

"He can't be too happy about that, especially not on the first day of the show," Patti agreed.

In front of the audience a blindfolded girl drew two names out of a hat. Bill had explained earlier that the couples were selected this way to avoid the possibility of "fixing" a show by briefing couples on their trivia questions ahead of time.

One pair of names was Patti and Alex. The other competitors turned out to be the young couple she'd noticed in the dressing room.

"Too bad," Alex said. "I would have liked a chance to watch this show in action first."

Bill gestured them to one of the brightly painted contestant counters. Theirs was yellow, the other one blue.

Everything on the set seemed to have been daubed with poster paints, Patti noted. The gleaming whites and brilliant accents hurt her eyes in the glare of the lights.

Appearing in a game show was always so different from watching it on TV, she reflected as she glanced around. Sitting at home, you didn't realize how far apart everything was—she was glad she had good eyesight to read the question board.

At a cue the audience and crew fell silent. A blare of taped music announced the opening credits, and then the cameras closed in on Argo Galoof.

"Hey, hey, hey!" he cried, and Patti winced. She much preferred the usual game show host's smooth if somewhat plastic charms, but *Lady Luck* had become a hit with a comedian host, so clearly its spin-off was following suit. "This is Argo Galoof, and welcome to *Double Luck*!"

After a few words about the fabulous cash prizes to be won, Argo introduced the contestants. "Alex Greene here is president of his own optical company and vice mayor of Citrus Grove. What do you do for fun, Alex?"

Patti blushed at the idiocy of the question, wishing she'd never put Alex in this awkward situation. But he didn't seem bothered by it in the least.

"I like to go sailing and I like to swim," he said. "And I love to win games."

"Sounds great! And now to Patti. Hello, Patti! It says here that you teach exercise to senior citizens." He clutched one hand to his heart. "Don't you have to keep the paramedics standing by?"

"We're trying to avoid heart attacks, not cause them." She kept a pleasant expression on her face.

Mercifully, Argo moved on to the young couple, who were introduced as the owners of a hobby shop and who admitted that their own favorite hobby was sleeping. "And now for round one!"

As the question board began flashing its lights and the taped music swelled again, Patti's nervousness subsided to be replaced by a burst of excitement.

It was a familiar response, the same one she'd had on the previous game shows—her hearing and vision seemed to sharpen and her mind cleared of all other considerations. The rippling tension of Alex's body beside her revealed that he shared her anticipation.

"And now—our contestants will press the buttons in front of them," Argo said. "That'll juice up the old computer—and who knows what happens next?"

The other couple received two deuces among their five cards, while Patti and Alex didn't have anything that scored.

Both teams decided to play for three new cards. "We'll keep the jack and the queen, since they're high," Alex suggested, and Patti agreed.

Although they answered the questions correctly, they drew no useful cards, and the younger couple won the round.

"We'll be right back for round two, following this message!" Argo boomed.

During the brief commercial break, the makeup woman touched up Patti's nose. "Glare," she explained.

"Well, there are two more rounds to go." Alex frowned, staring at the question board. "We just had some bad luck. But we got all three of our questions right, and they only got one."

Sure enough, Patti and Alex won the second round with three nines.

"Well, now, folks, things are really shaping up around here!" crowed Argo. "Whoever wins round three wins the match—and ten thousand dollars to go with it!"

Patti and Alex exchanged glances. She could feel the electricity crackling between them. Who would have expected Alex to get this excited about winning a contest?

In the final round he correctly named the capital of Tunisia—Tunis—and their card turned out to be a heart, which they needed for a flush. They'd won!

As soon as the segment was over, Patti hurried to the dressing room to change into another outfit. A few minutes later the woman they'd defeated came back to collect her clothes.

"I'm sorry we couldn't both win," Patti said, combing her hair.

"Me, too," the woman agreed, "but at least the consolation prizes are really nice. A camera, a year's supply of laundry detergent, and a gift certificate for fifty dollars in jewelry—that's not bad."

It became evident in the second match that Alex and Patti were on a roll. They won all three rounds.

Twenty thousand dollars so far—ten thousand apiece! Patti could hardly believe it! She grinned as she changed into a lavender skirt and blouse set. The prize money would really give her budget a boost.

Plus they had the chance to win not only an additional ten thousand, but five thousand more than that if, as undefeated triple champions, they answered a final trivia question.

Their competitors for the final game turned out to be Jerry and his wife, Evelyn.

Jerry obviously had been looking forward to the "meet the contestants" part of the show. As soon as Argo Galoof introduced him as a refrigerator salesman, Jerry boomed out, "That's right, and you know what I'm famous for? I once sold an icebox to an Eskimo! No kidding!"

"Really," Argo muttered, and turned to Evelyn. "So you operate your own knitting business at home . . ."

"She's the purl of my life!" crowed Jerry. "You know, knit one, purl two . . ."

"And now on with our show," said Argo Galoof with a pained smile.

Patti and Alex won the first round. Jerry and Evelyn took the second. During the commercial break, Alex whispered, "We've got to win this one. Otherwise, poor Argo is going to be stuck with Jerry for another segment."

"Okay, you've convinced me," Patti said. "Let's win it."

On the initial cards, Patti and Alex had a pair of tens but Evelyn and Jerry had three sevens.

"That's going to be tough to beat," Alex muttered.

Jerry drew the first question—which movie won the Best Picture Oscar in 1977?

"Uh—*Every Which Way But Loose?*" he said.

"Sorry." Argo didn't look the least bit sorry, and passed the question on to Patti and Alex.

"*Annie Hall*," Patti responded quickly. She loved Woody Allen movies.

The computer flashed the card they'd drawn—a seven. Useless to them, but it would have given Evelyn and Jerry an almost unbeatable four-of-a-kind.

Both couples were able to answer their next questions, and qualify for a draw. But neither drew a card that improved their showing.

Alex squeezed Patti's hand behind the counter, out of sight of the cameras. She could feel the tension in his arm and realized that he was as dead set on winning as she was.

The final question. Jerry and Evelyn got first crack at it: Which state is nicknamed the Hawkeye state?

Evelyn tried to speak but Jerry cut her off. "Ohio!" He beamed with pride. Evelyn was shaking her head.

"Too bad! Ohio's the Buckeye state!" Argo didn't even pretend to look sympathetic. "Back to you, Patti and Alex!"

Alex glanced at Patti. She widened her eyes slightly to show she didn't know the answer. "Iowa," he said with a trace of uncertainty.

"Iowa it is!" Argo said, and the scoreboard displayed their final card—a ten. Patti and Alex had won the final match!

The camera cut quickly away from the stunned Jerry and his tight-lipped wife, who looked as if she wanted to clobber him. "Congratulations," Argo was saying. "When we come back, we'll have one final trivia question for you—worth an additional five thousand dollars!"

The losing couple were escorted off the set. "They shouldn't ask those damn trick questions," Jerry grumbled.

His wife glowered at him.

The break ended quickly and Argo returned amid a roll of drums. "The final question—who won the only gold medal for the United States at the 1968 winter Olympics in Grenoble, France?"

It was Alex's turn to look blank. Patti couldn't resist jumping up and down in uncontained glee as she answered, "Peggy Fleming! I love ice skating!"

"I'll bet you do," said Argo.

Patti flung her arms around Alex and kissed him. Only after she stepped back and saw his expression of mingled pleasure and embarrassment did she realize what she'd done.

Embracing him in front of the television cameras—would he ever live it down? She felt herself flushing bright red.

Amid the staff's congratulations, she and Alex signed the appropriate forms, promising to pay their state and federal income tax on the winnings. Thirty-five thousand dollars—half for each of them!

The show would air in about a month. Alex promised to tape it on his video machine so they'd have a permanent record. He didn't look in the least abashed about the on-camera embrace.

As she gathered her extra clothes together, Patti let her thoughts drift to what she'd do with the money. A new car for sure—her old one had almost a hundred thousand miles on it...

"I think we should go out to celebrate." Alex had followed her into the room and took her zipper bag to carry it. "Don't you?"

"Oh, yes!"

They agreed that she'd follow in her car, and after some consideration they decided to have dinner at one of the restaurants on board the *Queen Mary* in Long Beach.

"I haven't been there in years," Patti admitted. "I did all the tourist sights when I first moved to southern California, but I've never gone back."

After the half-hour journey through the growing twilight, they parked in the vast lot that served both the *Queen Mary,* permanently at anchor, and its new neighbor, the *Spruce Goose.*

"I'll have to come back some day and tour the *Goose,"* Patti said, waving toward the mammoth airplane that had been intended to serve as an aerial troop ship but had only been flown once, by its designer, Howard Hughes.

Something wet dropped onto her hand. "Oh, darn, it's sprinkling," she said.

"Then let's get under some cover." Alex hurried her toward the ship. "What sort of food are you in the mood for?"

"What's the choice?" she asked, loping along as fast as she could in her high heels.

"Well . . ." They reached a covered ramp and he guided her up to the elevator. From this angle, the vast ship resembled a huge hotel, which was indeed what it had become.

"There's a restaurant that specializes in English food, and another that features seafood, and a steak-and-seafood house," said Alex. "What'll it be?"

"English food sounds interesting," Patti said.

"Done."

They stepped out of the elevator into a lobby, and Alex led her through a maze of hallways. The interior of the ship was filled with strolling, well-dressed couples. Here and there a small shop displayed dresses or jewelry—expensive souvenirs.

"Wouldn't it be fun to take a cruise?" she said.

"We can afford to. With what we've won." He steered her around a group of tourists who were listening to a guide.

"The *Queen Mary* carried eight hundred thousand troops during World War II," the guide was saying.

They passed out of earshot. "Couldn't we stop and listen?" Patti asked.

"It's a three-hour tour," Alex said. "Believe me, I know. Remember Sponsor-a-Kid Day?"

"Sure." Patti had participated in the event last summer, in which Citrus Grove residents were asked to take an underprivileged child to some cultural event or museum. "I took two little girls to the Natural History Museum."

"And I brought three junior high school boys to the *Queen Mary* and the *Spruce Goose*." Alex shook his head at the memory. "They loved it, but they certainly wore me out."

They'd reached the Lord Nelson restaurant. The walls were, like the rest of the ship, wood-paneled, and the atmosphere subdued and mellow, like an English supper club.

They ordered wine and opened their menus.

"Would you care to try the steak-and-mushroom pie? Or perhaps steak-and-kidney?" Alex said.

"Prime rib sounds a little more appealing," she admitted. "Isn't it wonderful to be able to afford all this? What are you going to buy with your winnings, Alex?"

He looked up startled. "Buy?"

"Well, you won seventeen thousand five hundred dollars," she reminded him.

"Oh, that's right." He chuckled. "All I could think about was beating that pompous fellow so poor Argo Galoof wouldn't have to put up with him for another show."

The waiter came by to bring the wine and take their orders, and then Patti said, "You still haven't told me what you plan to do with the money."

He took a sip of wine. "Donate it to the Help Center. They can certainly use it."

Patti felt a twinge of guilt. Maybe she ought to donate her winnings, too.

Then she remembered that her car was likely to break down any day, and that she couldn't afford to make payments.

"I'm going to donate mine to a worthy cause, too," she said. "Me."

To her relief, Alex refrained from any comment about social responsibility. "Sounds reasonable."

"You actually seemed to enjoy yourself today," she said. "I was surprised."

"I enjoy a challenge," he agreed. The waiter brought their salads, and he picked up his chilled fork.

"Is that what I am?" Patti asked.

"A challenge? I suppose you are." He studied her thoughtfully. "But that's not why I'm attracted to you."

"Oh?" She pretended an interest in her salad.

"You're different from the other women I've met," Alex said. "Oh, I suppose everyone is unique in some way or another, but you intrigue me."

Patti wasn't sure how to respond. "The way I grew up, a girl wasn't supposed to be 'different' or 'intriguing.' She was supposed to blend into the background. They called it making life run smoothly. Like a waiter is supposed to do."

"Are you sure you're being fair to your parents?" Alex said. "What I mean is, you haven't really had much contact with them since you've left home. Mostly you remember them the way they seemed to you as a teenager. Maybe if you looked closely, you'd see other sides to them that you hadn't noticed before."

Patti traced circles on the tablecloth with the tip of her fork. "I'm not sure they want to see me."

"Oh, come on, they're your parents." His tone crackled with disbelief.

She tossed her head defiantly. "This isn't all in my imagination, Alex. Their thirtieth anniversary is the weekend after next. Mom mentioned something in her last letter about a party, but she didn't give me any details and I haven't received an invitation."

"Maybe they're waiting for you to call and ask," Alex suggested.

"Maybe." Patti blinked back an unexpected tear. "It hurts to think they wouldn't want me at their own anniversary party. I've always longed to have them approve of me. I admire my sister—in her own quiet way, Ingrid manages to do what she wants and make it seem as if she's being obedient at the same time. I can't do that. I always shoot my mouth off or put my foot in it, somehow."

"I'm sure they want you there," Alex said. "Maybe your invitation was lost in the mail. It does happen, you know. Or maybe your parents assumed you knew you were to be included."

Their food arrived, and they began eating. The prime rib was delicious.

"I suppose I could call," Patti said. "But frankly, I'm apprehensive about going. Every time I see them, I end up feeling depressed."

He paused between bites. "I could go with you."

"You could?" she said in surprise.

"After all, I'm the man you hugged on national television," Alex teased.

"Well, if I hear from them and if I decide to go, I'll consider it. But right now, let's enjoy our victory," Patti said.

After dinner they strolled arm in arm through the ship. Outside, the rain had intensified into a heavy downpour.

They stood at a porthole, looking out. They were in a secluded corner, with no one around.

Alex's breath soothed across her hairline and he bent, brushing his nose across her temple. The unexpected contact filled her with silvery arrows of longing.

Then the point of his tongue found the rim of her ear, tracing the shell-like whorl. Instinctively, Patti's arms curved around his neck and they stood there, holding each other. She brushed her cheek against his, feeling the prickly hint of an incipient beard.

Their mouths met, parted, rediscovered each other. His teeth were polished and smooth beneath her tongue. They teased each other with licks and darts; she pulled back, and he followed, drawing her into a deep embrace that echoed all the way down to her toes.

"Somebody might see us," she whispered reluctantly.

"How would you like to spend a night on a ship?" he asked.

As if on cue, the rain gusted hard against the porthole. It would be dangerous to drive all the way back to Citrus Grove in this downpour.

"All right," she agreed. "I suppose it would be safest for us to stay."

But inside, she knew it wouldn't be safe at all.

- 6 -

THE STATEROOM WAS large and dignified, done in wood with rich maroon accents. It looked to Patti like a bedroom from an old world mansion, except for the porthole at the far side.

They'd tried to get two rooms, but there was a convention on board, and this had turned out to be the only room available.

Looking around, Patti wondered if it wouldn't be wiser to drive home in the rain, after all.

Before she could say anything, Alex slipped his arm around her waist. "I'm glad we have this chance to talk, to be together," he said. "There's something about having the rain beating against the window that makes me feel like telling ghost stories."

"Did you do that when you were a kid?" Patti asked, sinking into an upholstered chair. "My mother used to read me stories on rainy days when I was little—and it rains a lot in San Francisco—but she stopped as soon as I was old enough to read to myself."

Alex removed his shoes and sat against the headboard, his long legs stretched out across the coverlet. "We'd come back from sailing on Cape Cod and have a clambake on the beach. We'd sit around the fire, my parents, my brother, and I, and tell each other grim tales about the ghosts of vengeful sailors."

"It sounds like fun," she said, unable to hide a trace of envy. "Whenever we did anything as a family, it was organized down to the last detail. Sometimes I felt like we were going on a military expedition. Once we went to a carnival and we took our own food so we wouldn't get sick on cotton candy, and a change of shoes because we were going to visit someone afterward and Mom said we'd get all dusty on the fairway."

"I suppose that does make sense, depending on how you look at it," he observed.

"Well, maybe," she admitted. "I wonder how much of it was my own perception. I was trying so hard to please Mom and Dad that I probably took the rules more seriously than I had to."

"Are you cold?" Alex asked.

"A little." She hadn't noticed before, but she was shivering slightly.

"I don't know about you," Alex said, "but I'm getting under the covers. You can turn around if you're shy."

He began unbuttoning the cuffs of his shirt. Feeling awkward, Patti stood up and walked to the porthole and stared out at the rain-drenched parking lot.

"How sad everything looks in the rain," she reflected. "It reminds me of San Francisco; of my parents. I always wanted to have the perfect American family—like the ones on television. Parents who understood me, and problems that could be resolved in half an hour."

"I used to have a crush on Annette Funicello," Alex admitted.

"You did?" She turned around in astonishment and

saw that he was in bed, his pants and shirt lying neatly folded on a chair.

"Don't tell me you didn't have a crush on some actor," he challenged.

"Well..." She'd never revealed this to anyone. "Captain Kirk, actually."

"You mean on *Star Trek*?" His eyes shone with amusement.

"I imagined having a father like that—always fair and just and understanding," Patti said. "And of course handsome, too."

"That's quite a tall order to live up to." Alex's words seemed to carry a double meaning.

"You think that's what I'm looking for in a man, too?" she asked, sitting on the edge of the bed. She really did feel cold, but she didn't dare go to bed. Could she sleep on the carpet? But what would she use for covers?

"Excuse me for asking, but what the hell are you doing?" Alex asked.

"Trying to figure out where I'm going to sleep." She eyed the upholstered chair. She'd fallen asleep once in a chair at home and awakened with a stiff neck that hurt for two days.

"How about the bed?" he suggested.

"Yes, but you're in it."

He considered for a moment. "I'll make you a deal."

"What?"

"We'll go to sleep—in the same bed. Actually sleep. I promise not to do anything you don't want me to do, although I won't make any promises beyond that."

Suddenly Patti saw the humor of the situation. Here they were, a grown man and woman, primly bargaining over their sleeping arrangements.

"Sure, why not?" She kept her voice light. "As long as you're not the type who steals the covers."

"Hearts, yes; covers, no," he quipped. "I'll even let

you use the bathroom first."

"Okay."

The bathroom turned out to be old-fashioned, with a high tub and tile floor, but everything worked, including—thank goodness—the hot water.

With no nightgown, Patti had to content herself with her slip, a lacy wisp that hid very little. After taking off her clothes, she finger-brushed her teeth and then wrapped a bath towel around her shoulders for an added touch of propriety.

Opening the bathroom door, she found Alex waiting outside. He gave a loud wolf whistle.

"I like your ensemble," he said. "Except for the towel."

"The latest thing in shawls," she shot back on her way, rapidly, to the safety of the covers.

A few minutes later the lights flicked out and she felt the bedsprings sink beneath Alex's weight.

Patti huddled on her side of the bed, as close to the side as she dared, feeling ridiculously childish and overcome by embarrassment.

She'd never thought of herself as inhibited, but she certainly was about some things, she admitted to herself now—such as getting in bed with a man.

"Your feet are cold," Alex murmured.

She realized with a start that she'd instinctively pressed her chilly toes into the warmth of his leg. "Oh. I'm sorry." She withdrew them.

"How about a trade?" he suggested, his voice low and mysterious in the dark.

"What do you mean?"

By way of response, a pair of icy hands pressed into her stomach. Patti let out a yelp and grabbed his wrists, at the same time kicking out.

They wrestled playfully, sputtering and laughing as first one, then the other managed to shelter a half-frozen foot or hand against the other's heated flesh.

Alex caught Patti's wrists without warning and lifted

her arms over her head, his body simultaneously covering hers, and his mouth meeting her own willing one.

All thought of self-defense vanished as she succumbed to the intoxicating contact. No longer afraid of anything, Patti answered his kisses with her own, their tongues teasing each other until desert fire raced through her nerve endings.

She felt him trace the line of her cheekbones, chin, and lips. A butterfly kiss touched her mouth and forehead.

The base of her jaw proved to be remarkably sensitive, sparking tremors that jolted her body strongly enough to register on the Richter scale. Next, his fingers found their way to the hollow of her throat, where his tongue worked moist magical circles.

Now Alex lifted her hands, one at a time, feeling the delicate bones of the wrist and massaging her shoulders gently. Patti's remaining tensions poured out through her fingertips, leaving her body weak as a sleeping kitten.

Alex shifted her onto her side so he could rub the muscles of her back and ease away the aches of the day. It was remarkable, the close connection between pain and pleasure, she reflected as the sore muscles twinged beneath his strokes.

"I promised I wouldn't go any further without your permission." His voice sounded hoarse.

"I know . . ." She swallowed, wanting more and yet not ready for it. "Can't we just snuggle?"

A sigh answered her. "If that's the way you want it."

"I do." Patti rested her cheek against his shoulder. It was hard now to remember ever having been intimate with Mark; she was sure it had been nothing like this. Vaguely she remembered a spark of passion, a series of all-too-quick encounters, and an aftertaste of disappointment.

With Alex she felt different, as if he were a friend and confidante. If only things could always be this way, without the stresses and conflicts of everyday life. But she knew better.

"What are you thinking?" Alex asked.

"It's too bad real life can't be this way," she said. "But we're just playing tonight, aren't we? You don't have to worry about your duties and I don't have to worry about my freedom. We can just be together."

"It could be like that all the time." He propped himself up on one elbow.

"No." Patti shook her head. "This is neutral territory."

Alex laughed. "It sounds like we're engaged in a war."

He had a point. "But in a sense we are, aren't we? We both want the same thing, but we each want it to be our way."

"Only I'm the one who's right," he teased.

"Oh?"

"You've been running away from your childhood for years," Alex said. "It's time to stop and take a second look. Maybe things weren't as bad as you imagined."

"And maybe they were worse." The subtle pressure of his leg resting atop her ankle flooded Pattie with restlessness, with wanting more of him. "Maybe we should go to sleep now."

"Do you think we can?" His voice was low, challenging.

"Sure. Watch me."

She closed her eyes and pretended to sleep.

"Are you sure you wouldn't like another back rub?" Alex whispered.

She tried keeping quiet, but he merely waited. She could sense his nearness, his expectancy, and finally she glared up at him. "That isn't all you have in mind, now, is it?"

"Allow me to demonstrate." He rolled her gently onto her stomach and began to probe her tensions. An electricity flowed from his hands to her body, and after a few minutes Patti allowed him to explore the muscles of her legs.

Then it was her turn to massage him, enjoying the solid feel of his body beneath her hands. Gradually the kneading turned into stroking, and then they were in each others' arms.

The rain had started again, and the pattern sounded to Patti like the throb of primitive drumbeats. Desire danced to life within her.

Alex found her mouth again, making himself at home there in a long series of kisses. At the same time his hands played magically across her breasts.

"I want you," he murmured hoarsely. "So much, Patti."

Lightning crackled between them, and the storm that raged within the room had nothing to do with the rain streaming down outside.

Patti forgot her reservations, giving way to a torrent of feelings that were newborn at that moment, erupting from some previously unknown depths of her being.

Just when she thought she would explode, Alex whispered, "There's no hurry, my love. You've barely been awakened."

So he knew, somehow, that she'd never had these sensations before. How could it be that he, the conservative one, was so unrestrained while she, the independent soul, had newly been released from a prison of ignorance?

He renewed his embrace with tantalizing slowness. Patti felt herself flowing into him, a current of steamy water passing from her existence into his and then back once more.

Patti found herself seeing him with unusual clarity—the wonder and eagerness on his face, the powerful muscles of his arms and shoulders, the hair curling along his chest.

And then they were united in passion, both writhing

with their need for each other. The time for leisurely exploration was past. Rain slammed against the porthole and thunder shook the room, but they were nothing beside the drumming of her own heart.

The tight control he'd exercised before had fled entirely. Alex cried out with joy, the deep rasping noise thrilling through Patti in a primitive paean of triumph. This was her man; he needed her, and she was satisfying him in the most basic way a woman can reach a man. She was drowning, floating, dying, being born.

They reached the peak at the same time, hauling each other over the edge, almost violent in their longing. An earthquake ravaged Patti's body; wave after wave of pleasure shocked through her, blotting out all other awareness until at last she and Alex collapsed in a heap together.

Sometime later—she must have fallen asleep, she realized—Alex stirred, waking her.

"Is something wrong?" she murmured.

"No, I . . . thought I'd take a shower." He planted a light kiss on the tip of her nose. "No need for you to get up."

"Oh!" Her eyes flew open. "I'll come, too."

He flicked on the bedside lamp, revealing their golden bare skin, her rounded curves against his hard length. Smiling, he pulled back the covers and lay propped on one elbow, taking in the sight of her nudity.

"It's cold!" Patti protested, finding the discarded towel and pulling it around her shoulders. "Let's go take that shower."

She darted into the bathroom, and he followed more slowly. A hot stream of water restored Patti to affability, and she splashed him lightly as he joined her.

They soaped each other, playful as two seals. She washed his back and chest, and then her hands ventured lower.

"Hey!" Alex caught her around the waist and drew her up for a soapy kiss.

Patti had never felt so free, so completely at ease with a man before. She'd never imagined she could react this way, swaying against him deliberately to tantalize his senses, arching so the hot water danced across both their bodies at the same time.

"Wench," he whispered hoarsely.

She could do to him what he'd done to her, Patti thought as her hands began kneading the muscles of his neck and shoulders.

Bathed in damp heat, she investigated him thoroughly—the newly familiar bulges and lines of his body, the light-brown curly hair that covered much of his chest, arms, and legs; the sensitive places that drew a moan when she touched them.

"Maybe we'd better get out of here before we drown," he muttered.

Patti flicked off the jets as Alex wrapped them both in the skimpy motel towels. They took turns drying each other with sensuous circling motions that brought desire back in full force.

They adjourned to the bed. The sheets felt cool at first beneath their slightly moist bodies, but their ardor quickly heated it to sauna temperatures.

"My turn," Patti said, pushing Alex down flat onto his back.

It was the first time she'd felt comfortable taking the lead in lovemaking; with Mark there had been no question of that. He always insisted on being in control.

Alex shivered beneath her caresses, called out her name, reached for her, and then subsided amid the sensations she was delivering.

Was she falling in love with him? At this moment the possibility seemed quite delicious. There was nothing in the world but her and him and this room and the rain softly pattering down outside.

When Patti's attentions had driven him past endurance, Alex pulled her on top of him and united them once again. "I've never... known anyone... like you," he gasped.

Again the storm burst within the room and thundered to a climax, and then ebbed away.

"Oh, Patti, my precious, my own." Alex cuddled her against him. "You are one very special woman."

Basking in the glow of happiness, she fell asleep.

"There's no hurry getting home today, is there?" he asked as they checked out of the *Queen Mary* the next morning.

"Oh, anytime next year would be fine," Patti said.

"My sentiments exactly."

They left her car in the parking lot and drove to Venice beach. The day was sharp and bright, as southern California days usually are after a storm. The sunlight had an unusual clarity to it, and looking inland you could see the deeply etched crags of the mountains ringing Los Angeles.

For breakfast Alex had chosen a small café with tables outside on a patio, half a block from the beach. They picked up a newspaper on the way in.

Lingering over an indulgent breakfast of bacon, eggs, pancakes, and toast, Alex and Patti read to each other from the comic pages and debated the merits of the editorials.

Naturally, they disagreed on one calling for the elimination of investment credits and other tax breaks for the wealthy.

"It's not fair that poor people have to pay a higher percentage of their income in taxes," Patti pointed out.

"That's true—but you have to give people an incentive for investing their money," Alex said. "A lot of businesses are marginal, but they provide jobs. It's only because of the tax breaks that a lot of them exist."

Finally they moved on to the less controversial feature section.

"It's a good thing today's Saturday," Alex said. "If we had the entire Sunday editorial section to argue about, we'd be here all week."

"That doesn't sound so bad," Patti said.

They looked up at a noise on the sidewalk that ran alongside the café. Two teenagers whizzed by on roller skates, making the clattering sound that had caught their attention.

"That looks like fun." Patti finished her blueberry muffin.

"Yes, it does," Alex said. "Shall we?"

"Shall we what?"

"Go roller-skating." He lifted one eyebrow, daring her.

"Sure." Patti grinned. "Why not?"

Along the broad sidewalk that ran beside the beach, they found a rental store and exchanged their shoes for two pairs of skating boots.

"These things have really improved since I was a kid." Patti held onto the counter for support as she stood up. "We had those clunky metal wheels that you clamped on to the rims of your shoes."

"These are a lot lighter, and safer," Alex agreed. "Well, are we going to stand here all day discussing the merits of modern technology?"

Patti gave him a playful poke in the ribs and skated out the door of the shop, nearly colliding with a bicyclist. The rider shot her an unfriendly look and pedaled on.

"Hey! We're supposed to be a team!" Alex caught up and rested his arm on her waist.

"You might not want to stay too close to me," Patti warned. "I have a feeling I'm going to fall down a lot." She glanced at her cotton skirt, hoping that at least it would shield her knees from scrapes.

"Then I'll have to catch you," said Alex.

They wove slowly along the sidewalk between children in strollers, elderly couples on bicycles and oversize tricycles, teenagers in outrageously revealing bathing suits, and other skaters.

One boy circled around them, performing wheelies. "Very good," Alex said.

"Yeah, man, you should see me break dance!" The boy glowed under the praise and skated away.

"Friendly place," Patti noted.

"That's one of the things I like about California," Alex said. "At the beach you feel like everybody's your neighbor."

They stopped at midday for a lunch of frozen yogurt. Alex picked chocolate with chocolate sprinkles, and Patti selected strawberry flavor with fresh strawberries on top.

"I'm not entirely convinced this is good for me," she admitted, finishing her dish. "But who cares?"

Finally they returned the skates and sank onto a bench, staring over the beach at the placid expanse of the Pacific Ocean. Catalina Island rose in the distance.

"It's been a long time since I've taken a whole day just to enjoy myself," Alex admitted.

With a start, Patti realized that was true of her, too. Even though she'd avoided tying herself down to a full-time job, she didn't feel comfortable just lazing around. Instead, she always seemed to be helping Irene with a project or chauffeuring one of her senior citizens to the supermarket or baby-sitting Jennifer.

"I guess we bring out the child in each other," she said.

They stayed at the beach until dark, browsing through shops, nibbling at hot dogs and french fries, and teasing each other like teenagers.

Then they picked up her car and drove to Citrus Grove. Patti stopped at her house to change, feeling as if she'd been away for a long time—on a voyage of discovery.

At Alex's house they discovered they were too tired to do more than nestle together and watch a videotape of *Victor/Victoria,* one of Patti's favorite movies.

I think I love him, she realized after they turned off the lights and lay side by side in his king-size bed.

It was too bad, she reflected as her eyelids grew heavier, that life wasn't like a day at the beach. You couldn't just skate your way around life's obstacles.

Her thoughts drifted back to the night they'd met. Alex in a three-piece suit at City Hall. Alex sitting with the other council members, looking stiffly dignified.

How different he'd been today, loose and easy and joyful. Part of him is like me, Patti thought. But what about the other part?

Then she fell asleep.

- 7 -

ON SUNDAY MORNING Alex mixed pancake batter in his immaculate kitchen, sliced up strawberries, and whipped a carton of cream.

"Belgian waffles," he announced, scooping a stack from the specially designed grill-press onto Patti's plate.

She breathed in the delicious smells and, at the same time, drank in the sight of him, more handsome than ever in jeans and a green pullover. "You sure know how to spoil a girl."

"I take it out in trade." His hand slid up her blue jean-clad leg toward the thigh.

"Oh?" Pattie paused with a forkful of waffle halfway to her mouth. "On a full stomach?"

"Well, maybe after you've digested a bit," he returned with mock gravity.

She laughed. It was good to be here, in his airy house. Being together felt like the most natural thing in the world.

The current that flowed between them during breakfast was steady and reassuring. They touched each other naturally, awakening responses and not feeling any immediate need to act on them.

"I wish I weren't going to be so busy this week," Alex said. "I've got one meeting or another almost every night."

"What's going on?" Patti asked.

"Some of it's business, some of it's the council," he said. "And I'm meeting with a couple of police officers to get more information on poker parlors. The vote's coming up a week from tomorrow."

"I hope you change your mind," Patti said.

"We don't have to agree on everything, you know." Absentmindedly, he fingered the crease in his jeans. They'd been ironed, Patti noted.

"The problem is that we agree on most of the little things—what to eat for breakfast, whether to go roller-skating," she said. "It's the big things that worry me."

"They can be worked out." His tone was a bit too confident for Patti's liking. She had a feeling that he meant things could be worked out if she would only come to her senses and see things his way.

They finished breakfast and went outside to relax on a pair of lounge chairs. Despite a slight nip in the air earlier that morning, the day was warming up quickly.

"Do you ever have skinny-dipping parties?" Patti teased, surveying the pool area with its high, vine-draped walls.

"Only when I'm seeking the nudist vote." Alex pulled off his shirt, revealing a tempting bronze expanse. He looked like a Greek god, bold and seminude.

Suddenly it dawned on Patti that although they were outdoors, this really was a private setting. The semi-isolated canyon by itself would have kept intruders away, and the high walls added to her sense of security.

Spontaneously, Patti untucked her own blouse and

began unbuttoning it. "That looks like a good idea."

Alex stared in surprise, apparently not believing she really meant to go through with it. With a touch of defiance, Patti pulled off her top and undid her bra.

"There." She lay back in the chaise lounge. "Now we can be twins."

"Hardly." Alex chuckled.

It felt strangely arousing, the sun beating down on her bare breasts. Patti could hear Alex's breath coming quicker.

"You know," he observed after a moment, "it's easy to get a burn if you don't take proper precautions."

"Did you have something particular in mind?" she challenged.

"As a matter of fact . . ." He retrieved a bottle of suntan lotion from under his chair and came to sit beside her.

A thin stream of cold lotion spurted onto Patti's chest, followed by Alex's strong hands massaging it into her skin. A great earth-richness opened up inside her, like a meadow responding to spring warmth.

"You know," he murmured, "it's going to look odd, having a tan line stop right at your waist. Maybe we ought to get rid of the rest of these silly clothes."

A smooth gesture left her nude in the sunlight.

Her heartbeat quickened as Alex shed his jeans and stood before her, golden and unclad. She let her gaze roam his well-shaped body.

He bent down and removed the pins from her hair so that it fell in a dark cloud across her shoulders. "You're stunning, my love."

As he stroked her hair, Patti smiled. "You certainly called my bluff—or should I say buff?"

He groaned at the pun. "I'm not one to shy away from a challenge."

From down the street came the rumble of a passing truck, reminding Patti that they were outdoors and completely undressed.

"I think we ought to go inside." She swung into a sitting position.

"Afraid?" he asked. "This yard is completely secluded. I made sure of that when I bought it; I like my privacy."

His words were reassuring but his hands were doing their best to overcome her resistance by less intellectual means.

"We're not actually going to make love out here," she whispered, half-scandalized and half-tempted.

"Why on earth not?" Then he added teasingly, "You know perfectly well Vice Mayor Greene wouldn't do anything that wasn't completely proper."

Firm hands on her shoulders pressed Patti back in the chaise, and Alex renewed his seductive attack.

She moved beneath him, lost in the sheen of sensuality that surrounded them. In the sunlight their skin gave off scents of rich amber that mingled into a heady aphrodisiac.

Alex was beautiful, uninhibited, marvelously constructed, and he knew how to use every inch of his magnificent body to best effect.

The harsh sound of his breathing told her that he shared her passion and soon, gently, he entered her. In her heightened state of sensitivity, Patti felt every movement quiver through her nervous system, until she was deliciously weak.

Finally her hands clutched his shoulders and she blossomed into a full ripeness, crying out with joy and hearing his answering gasp of pleasure.

They lay still for a moment before he lifted her and carried her into the heated swimming pool. Within its warm depths they nuzzled each other lazily.

From inside the house the phone began to ring. Alex hesitated and then, with a muttered oath, emerged from the pool, twisted a towel around his waist, and went inside.

Couldn't he just ignore it? Patti wondered with mild irritation. But, to be fair, she reminded herself that Alex was a member of the city council. When you took on a responsibility like that, you couldn't always do as you wished.

She climbed out of the pool and dried herself. It was only when she approached the house and heard the agitated edge to Alex's voice that she realized something was wrong.

Patti stepped inside and waited. She heard the caller addressed as "Sister Anna." So it was the nun who'd telephoned—but why?

A minute later Alex hung up and turned toward her. "Something's happened to Rosa Nunez," he said.

Patti's throat caught at the memory of that troubled young girl, dark hair falling across her face as she played cards in the church auditorium. "What is it?"

As he spoke, Alex led the way into the bedroom and dressed rapidly. "She was riding on the back of her boyfriend's motorcycle when he took a turn too fast and had a spill. Her head hit the pavement."

"Is—is she going to be all right?"

"They're not sure. She's still unconscious," he said, adding bitterly, "The boy walked away without a scratch."

Patti shivered, feeling helpless and angry. "Why did Sister Anna call you?"

"The family has no medical insurance," Alex said. "Medi-Cal won't cover everything."

Patti thought about her game show winnings. "I could help."

"That shouldn't be necessary." Alex's hand closed over hers in shared concern. "I plan to contribute and some of the Hispanic leaders in the community will want to help, I'm sure."

"There must be something I can do," Patti pleaded. "I feel as if I should have prevented it somehow—made more of an effort to befriend Rosa, or at least pointed out to her the dangers of seeing that guy—"

"Believe me, a lot of people tried, but you know how headstrong kids are at that age." Alex ran his hand through his hair. "They think they're invincible. And I can understand her frustration. She had to do all the cooking, baby-sitting, and housecleaning while her mother took care of the father and grandmother."

As he spoke he picked up his car keys.

"Are we going to the hospital?" Patti said.

"Not yet." He took a deep breath. "I'm going to call on some of the Hispanic leaders. I'd better drop you off at home; I'll come by later."

"I'll call Sister Anna," Patti said. "I'm sure the Nunez family can use some help at home, looking after the children and so on."

Alex nodded and jotted down the nun's phone number.

After he left her at home, Patti placed the call.

"Thank you so much for offering," Sister Anna said. "I have a list of numbers of people who might be able to assist. I was about to call them, but I feel I should go to the hospital to sit with Rosa. Maybe if you could—"

"—I'll be glad to take over," Patti assured her.

For the rest of the afternoon, she called every number on the list. By three o'clock she'd lined up people to take casseroles to the Nunez household, every meal for a week, as well as volunteer baby-sitters and Spanish-speaking companions who would tend Mr. Nunez while his wife stayed at their daughter's bedside.

As she made the arrangements, Patti drew up a chart with phone numbers and alternatives, so the Nunez family would know whom to call if a meal failed to materialize or a sitter couldn't make it.

She drove over to the family's house, now, a ramshackle, two-bedroom cottage south of the railroad tracks. The eldest son was trying to keep order among his screaming siblings, but, used to Rosa's attentions, they loudly ignored him.

Patti distracted the children with a fairy tale and soon had them settled down for a nap. By then, the first of her volunteers arrived.

She drove home pleased at what she'd accomplished but worried about Rosa. What if the girl were to die? Suffer permanent brain damage?

Perhaps Patti should go to the hospital. But Sister Anna had said that no visitors were allowed and that the waiting room was already overfilled with concerned friends.

Home again, trying to relax over a TV dinner, Patti found her thoughts returning to Alex.

The man was a puzzling mixture of stern uprightness and genuine caring. There were so many things about him to love, and yet her better judgment warned her off.

It was one thing for him to accept strange quirks in someone he was dating. But Patti knew enough about relationships—from her own experience—to realize that things changed once you got married.

Not that she expected Alex to become as overbearing and remote as Mark. But she knew he wouldn't be as easygoing as he'd been these last few days, either.

She would become his wife, a reflection of him, a sharer of his home. He'd want her to live up to his standards, just as her father always had. And she couldn't bear that kind of life again, no matter how much she loved Alex.

The doorbell rang. She speared a last potato puff, then went to answer it.

Alex leaned in the doorway, looking tired but pleased. "You're amazing," he said. "I went by the Nunez house and found everything in apple-pie order, including your chart tacked up on the wall."

"How's Rosa?" Patti asked.

"She's doing well. In fact, she roused for a few minutes, though the doctors say it may be another day or so before they know if there's been any brain damage." He came inside and sank onto the sofa while she hurried to pour him a cup of coffee.

"What about the medical bills?" She stirred cream and sugar into her cup.

"One of the doctors volunteered his services," Alex said. "Sister Anna had some emergency funds, and several businessmen in the community made anonymous donations."

"Including you?" she asked.

"If I answered that, it wouldn't be anonymous, would it?" Despite his weariness, his voice carried a teasing note.

Patti had a feeling she knew what he'd done with his winnings from *Double Luck*.

"You know," he said, "you have a real talent for getting things done."

"Oh?"

Alex drained his coffee cup. "There aren't many people who could have organized a week-long relief program in one afternoon."

"Sister Anna gave me the list," Patti said. "And I've gotten to know a lot of people in the community through my teaching. It wasn't hard."

"Yes, but you've got a real gift," he persisted. "You'd be quite a businesswoman if you put your mind to it. Frankly, I don't think you're making the best use of your talents."

"What do you mean?"

"I mean that teaching a few classes and appearing on game shows isn't really a career." He paused as if undecided, and then pushed on. "Look Patti, I know you're sensitive about this, but you're capable of achieving so much—"

"Oh, sure!" she snapped. Why did he have to try to force her into a mold, just when they'd been getting along so well? "I spent all day on the phone making arrangements because it was necessary, but let me tell you what

I really wanted to do. I wanted to spend the day holding Rosa's hand and comforting her mother. Just because I'm capable of organizing things doesn't mean that's how I want to spend my life, Alex!"

"Do you think any of us gets to do what we want all the time?" His weariness showed, but he pushed on. "Life isn't all fun and games, Patti."

"Do you think I don't know that?" She wished they weren't fighting, but something inside wouldn't let her give in. "I want to live my life my own way!"

"You won't be young forever," he persisted. "You've got to think about the future. Caring about others is important, and so is enjoying life, but that isn't enough. You've got to establish your place in society—"

"I don't need society!" Oh, how well she remembered her parents' warnings about keeping up appearances: always choosing the appropriate dress, watching your words, never smiling too broadly or frowning at the wrong moment. As if it didn't matter who you really were, only what impression you gave.

"How did we get into this fight?" Alex brushed his hand across his eyes. "Patti, I don't want to quarrel."

"Neither do I," she said miserably.

They were sitting across from each other, too far to touch. Their physical distance said more about their argument than any words.

"This morning..." Alex's expression softened. "Patti, there are a lot of good things between us."

"I know," she whispered, pain twisting her insides. She loved this man—oh, she did—it hurt even to admit it. For he might never accept her as she really was. And she couldn't force herself into a role simply to please him. It would destroy their feelings for each other, sooner or later.

The phone rang. Anxious that it might be some word about Rosa, Patti hurried to answer it. "Hello?"

The background hum told her immediately the call

was long distance. It was Ingrid, calling from Denver.

After the usual exchange of pleasantries, Ingrid said, "I thought you'd want to know that Mom and Dad's thirtieth wedding anniversary is a week from Friday. They're having a big party."

"I was wondering why I hadn't been invited," Patti said.

"Well, Mom seems to be under the impression that she did invite you," Ingrid said. "I'm just calling to fill in the details."

Patti took notes on a pad by the phone. "Do they really want me there?" she asked when her sister had finished. "I know you'd like to patch things up, but—"

"Honestly, they do," Ingrid insisted. "They love you and they miss you, even though they don't always act like it. I think you should go."

"I'm not sure," Patti said.

"Tom and I'll be there with the kids," Ingrid added. "We'd love to see you."

Patti smiled, thinking of her nephews. "I'd like that. But I have to give it some thought."

After her sister hung up, she filled Alex in on the conversation.

"I think you should go," he said. "It sounds like the perfect opportunity to make friends with them, as an adult."

"But they didn't even call me themselves!" Patti protested. "Ingrid's always trying to play peacemaker. It may have been her idea to invite me."

"I can't imagine any parents who wouldn't want both their daughters at their thirtieth anniversary party," Alex said. "You could fly up in the morning and come back the same night—and don't tell me you can't afford it. I'm sure your father could find room for you on one of his charter planes."

Patti sank onto the sofa. The timing was terrible, she thought. Here she was, poised on the verge of a complex relationship with Alex, torn by her need for him and her need for freedom. "I'm not sure I have the emotional stamina to face them just now."

"I could come along for moral support," Alex said. "In fact, I'd like to meet your parents."

The prospect of having him with her was somewhat reassuring—but a bit intimidating, too. Suppose he hit it off with her parents and took their side? Not that it seemed likely—Alex was far too loyal—but Patti couldn't help remembering the alliance between her family and Mark. Or perhaps they'd dislike him, and she'd find herself caught in the middle.

"I'll let you know," she said finally. "This really is difficult for me, Alex. Suppose things don't go well? Suppose my parents and I end up quarreling and spoiling their anniversary? I'd feel terrible."

"Don't underestimate yourself." He stroked beneath her chin, lifting her face toward him. "You're mature enough to avoid an argument if you want to. You don't have to let your parents get your goat, no matter what they do."

"I've never been good at holding in my feelings." Tears prickled near the surface of her eyes. Would she never have the closeness to her parents that she'd always longed for? Why couldn't they have been more like her, open and enthusiastic and willing to enjoy life?

"Whatever you decide, I promise not to pester you about it," Alex said, rising to leave. He paused in the doorway. "Patti, let's not allow these issues to come between us. We have something very special together."

She went into his arms, a tender, lingering embrace. There was a note of pleading in the way his lips found hers and tarried in a kiss.

"We'll . . . both have to do our best," she said.

"Yes." He clasped her hands for a moment before going out the door.

- 8 -

ON MONDAY, ROSA Nunez began to sit up and talk, and by Wednesday she was well enough to receive visitors. Sister Anna said on the telephone that the doctors now believed there was no permanent brain injury.

Alex and Patti met at the hospital that afternoon and went to Rosa's room together. They found her sitting in bed, thumbing restlessly through a romance novel.

Pulling up a chair, Patti took in the bruises that darkened Rosa's face. "You had a close call, didn't you? We were really worried."

"You were?" Rosa set down the book and looked at the two of them.

Patti nodded. "Tell me what the doctors say."

Rosa brought them up to date on her treatment, then added, "Sister Anna told me you both went on a game show and won a lot of money."

"As a matter of fact, it's scheduled to air next month," said Alex from where he leaned against the windowsill. "You should be home long before then."

"They said I could get out on Sunday." Rosa plucked at her blanket. "He was a real jerk, wasn't he?"

"Your friend?" Patti guessed.

A nod answered her. "I thought Jim loved me. But he hasn't come to see me once. And it was his fault. He was showing off." Rosa glared at the unseen boyfriend. "I could have been killed."

"What are you going to do now?" Patti asked.

"Do?"

"You're not just going to go home and disappear into a pile of diapers, are you?" she said.

Alex picked up the thread. "As a matter of fact, Rosa, the Help Center is starting a youth employment agency. Some of the local companies, including mine, are hiring teenagers part-time and giving them practical business experience. Would you be interested?"

"I could sure use the money," Rosa admitted.

"And you might find you have more talents than you realize," Alex continued. "Eventually, you could make a good salary. And we have a program where you can work part-time while you go to community college."

A light clicked on in Rosa's eyes, as if she were gazing into a future that suddenly looked brighter. "I always thought I'd get married right after high school," she said. "But it doesn't look like that's going to work out now." She appeared to be contemplating for a moment. "Do you think I could earn enough to have my own apartment?" she asked suddenly.

Alex smiled. "Eventually, sure," he said. "I'll tell you what. In a couple of weeks, when you're recovered, come and see me at Greene Optics and I'll find you an after-school job."

Rosa's eyes opened wide. "Gee, thanks, Mr. Greene!" Her gaze shifted to Patti. "You sure are lucky . . . to have a man like that," she finished shyly.

"So he tells me." Patti grinned. They chatted for a few more minutes, and Patti promised to come visit Rosa on Sunday when she got home.

Patti and Alex walked out of the hospital together. "That was kind of you, to offer to hire her," Patti said.

"Actually, I have a feeling she'll be an excellent employee," he said. "She's intelligent and eager. So you see, I was merely being selfish."

"Sure." Patti touched his arm. "You know, I've missed you."

"Not as much as I've missed you." He drew her close. "Frankly, I thought you might object."

"To your helping Rosa? Why on earth?" she asked.

"I was afraid you'd think I was trying to force her into a role." He rubbed his cheek against her hair. "And in a way I suppose I am."

"That's different," Patti said. "For one thing, she liked the idea, so you weren't pushing her."

"True," he conceded.

"Besides, she's in a dead-end situation. She doesn't have the skills and education yet to know what her options are. You were just showing her some possibilities," Patti went on. "I'm a different story."

"If you say so." Before she could reply, he changed the subject. "I'm afraid I've got an important client coming into town this weekend, from New York. I'll be meeting him and his wife at the airport Friday night and you're welcome to join us for dinner Saturday, although I warn you, we'll probably talk fiber optics and lasers."

"That's okay with me," she said.

The dinner turned out to be every bit as dull as Alex had warned. The client, a pale man in his mid-thirties named Marty, talked exclusively in numbers—dollar amounts and statistics—while his wife drank her way through three martinis. Patti did her best to look interested, wondering all the while how much of Alex's time was spent in meetings like this.

Alex seemed to be enjoying himself. Clearly he took

satisfaction from the challenge of persuading this man that Greene Optics offered the best quality in lasers for the best price.

Would life with Alex be like her marriage to Mark—evenings waiting home alone, or, only slightly better, evenings spent trying to pretend she wasn't bored by conversation about technical matters?

Perhaps she was being unfair, Patti told herself. After all, any businessman had to do a certain amount of entertaining clients.

It didn't help that Alex took her directly home afterward. "I promised to join Marty alone for a drink," he said. "And we may be out late. I don't want you to have to wait up for me."

"When are they leaving?" Patti asked with a sigh.

"Sunday night. I'm afraid I won't get a chance to see you before the council meeting," he said.

He kissed her, but clearly his mind was already racing forward to the business deal he hoped to conclude.

Patti tried to watch television, but it was hard to concentrate. She kept seeing flashes of Alex—roller-skating at Venice beach . . . sitting stiffly at the council meeting . . . offering Rosa Nunez a job . . . gleaming with enjoyment tonight as he faced a business challenge . . .

And there was still the matter of her parents' anniversary party to decide.

A part of her really did want to share the special occasion with them. Maybe finally, after all these years, they could come to some kind of understanding . . .

Maybe her parents could finally accept her as an individual, even though she wasn't the kind of conservative, conventional daughter they seemed to want . . .

But what if that wasn't the case? Patti and her parents had maintained a fragile truce these past few years, and she was glad to have at least this much of a relationship with them. Suppose somehow she disrupted their party, embarrassed them in front of their friends? They'd never forgive her . . .

Finally Patti went to bed and left the future to take care of itself.

Rosa was released from the hospital Sunday afternoon. Patti drove over to the cottage that evening with a bouquet of flowers.

"I don't know how to thank you," Mrs. Nunez said. A volunteer was tending the children, while another unloaded a hearty supper for the family. Sister Anna supervised the proceedings.

"I wish I could have done more." Patti glanced toward the bedroom. She'd stuck her head in to say hello, but Rosa was sleeping, and she knew the girl needed to rest. "Well, maybe I'd better go. I just wanted to be sure you were settled in all right. And please tell Rosa I came by."

Sister Anna walked her out to her car. "You know, you surprised me a little," the nun admitted.

"I did?" Patti paused outside the convertible, her mind still half-focused on the sleeping girl inside the house.

"When I first met you, at the church, I thought you were a kind-hearted person, but very happy-go-lucky—not the type of woman who would suit Mr. Greene," Sister Anna said.

Patti couldn't help laughing. "That's exactly what I thought the first time I ran into him."

"But I was wrong," the nun persisted. "You're exactly right for him. Perhaps it's none of my business, but I hope things work out between you. I think he's been looking for someone like you."

Remembering her reservations of the previous night, Patti swallowed hard. "Sister Anna, there are a lot of differences in the way Alex and I see things."

The nun folded her hands in front of her. "He drove us home from the hospital today—my car broke down and I called him at the last minute, and he came right over. Then afterward he spoke of you, briefly, but I could see the warmth in his eyes."

Patti looked down at the sidewalk, feeling her eyes fill with tears. Oh, yes, they cared about each other, but was it enough?

"I wish you both the best." The nun wore a faraway look. "And even if things don't turn out well, Patti, I hope you'll consider me one of your new friends."

"I'd like that very much." Patti clasped the woman's hands for a moment. "I admire how you devote yourself to others. I'm afraid I could never be that dedicated."

"My work provides its own rewards," Anna said. "Believe me, I get plenty back from the people I serve."

They said good-bye and parted with warm feelings.

Why had Sister Anna spoken to her this way? Patti wondered on her way home. Did the nun sense the problems between Patti and Alex?

She wondered what Sister Anna's life had been like before she entered the convent. Had she once loved someone, and lost him because they couldn't resolve their differences?

One of these days I'll take her out to lunch, Patti decided. She's definitely someone I want to know better.

Monday was the day of the council meeting, and it was difficult for Patti to concentrate on her work. Fortunately, her elderly pupils had a way of making their presence felt.

Because Halloween was only a few days away, many of them came to class dressed in costume, a hilarious assemblage of bright colors and fake jewelry.

They seemed to delight in ribbing each other: "That Jake, he's a real lady's man" (Jake was wearing a dress) ... "Now, Esther, she could charm a man right out of retirement" (Esther was wearing a ghoul mask from the dime store).

Several had apparently saved outfits from their youth—a flapper dress and beads, a zoot suit—but others had chosen disguises as animals or fairy-tale figures.

Zelda Roark, always the most original, wore a large box covered with contact paper cutouts designed to resemble a carton of Raisin Bran. Her head and leotard-clad arms stuck out through strategically placed holes.

"Did you make that yourself?" Patti asked as she snapped a tape into the cassette player.

"Well, I designed it, dear, but you know, my arthritis wouldn't let me do all the fine cutting." Zelda wiggled her fingers flirtatiously at a teenager who was escorting his grandmother. He grinned and winked back.

"At least you're already wearing your leotard and tights." Patti couldn't resist teasing her least athletic student. "Maybe you can warm up with us."

"Oh, it does my joints good just to watch," the lady countered, and plopped herself on a low table wide enough to accommodate her box.

Patti turned on the tape and began to stretch. "Reach high . . . that's right . . ."

What a scene everyone made, bobbing and kicking! As they turned to the music, a fairy godmother accidentally smacked a witch with her wand and was in turn swished by a lion's tail.

Before Patti knew it, the class was over. This time Irene had arranged to pick her up, and as a result, the two women made it to the city council meeting a good five minutes early.

Irene had left Jennifer at home with Paul this time, and the two friends gave each other moral support as they waited for the session to begin.

"I'm sure the ordinance will pass," Irene said. "We've got at least three of the five—and that's all we need. Unless Vice Mayor Greene changes somebody's mind. Or—" she added mischievously, "somebody changes his."

That didn't seem likely, Patti had to admit.

She tried not to stare as Alex took his place, his tall figure dominating the proscenium. He looked endearingly handsome, but very different from the man she'd made love to, sitting up there in his business suit.

His stern expression reminded her of the way her father had looked once when his company was hit with a nuisance lawsuit by a man who had gotten drunk and fallen down the steps of a charter flight.

She'd been helping out with some extra typing at her father's office that summer, and overheard the company lawyer explaining why they should pay off rather than go to court, even though the suit was unjustified.

Under pressure from his board of directors, her father finally gave in. But he was so furious at losing—especially since he believed he was right—that he stalked around in a foul temper for two days.

Patti's attention returned to the present as Alex's gaze swept the audience and lighted on her with a zing of contact. But he looked quickly away.

"I'm afraid I didn't have much success," she told Irene. "At changing his mind, anyway."

Her friend grinned. "Well, the world would be a dull place if everyone agreed on everything."

Patti wished she could share the same lighthearted spirit. If only she didn't have the nagging feeling that things might not work out tonight.

"What if we lose?" she asked Irene. "Would it really be so terrible?"

Her neighbor's expression sobered. "Well, we've managed to do without the money so far. But a lot of it would be going to the Help Center, and they really need it—the place is just getting established. They're in a very critical stage right now."

Patti wasn't enjoying the situation at all. Either way, somebody or something she cared about was going to lose. She had a feeling Alex wasn't going to take kindly to coming out on the short end, either.

That look on his face during dinner last night haunted her. Alex loved to win. Just like her father.

Patti chewed on her lip, wishing she could X-ray Alex's mind. Or maybe she was making too much of this. Somehow where he was concerned, she found it impossible to be objective.

The mayor called the meeting to order, and, as before, they went through the pledge of allegiance and the invocation.

Then the mayor introduced the issue of poker parlors.

"We heard from our citizen spokespersons at our previous meeting," he remarked. "Tonight the council members have done some research and arranged for expert testimony. Mrs. Franklin?"

The councilwoman called up an accountant who testified on the expected revenues, based on the experiences of other communities.

"That would certainly give a boost to our social services," Mrs. Franklin said after he'd finished. "Especially now that we're gathering so many of them under one roof."

The next person to speak was a woman from another city who lived next to a poker parlor. She attested to a lack of problems with either litter or any form of crime due to rigorous policing by the club management.

"In fact, I'd say the club is a lot better for the neighborhood than the restaurant that used to be there," she concluded. "We had all sorts of problems with noise, drunks, and excess traffic."

When it was Alex's turn, he called the police spokesman, Sergeant Vernon, to come forward.

"We've talked to the police in three other communities," the officer told the council. "They mentioned one incident in which a fight broke out between two patrons, resulting in superficial stab wounds."

"That could happen anywhere," Irene muttered in Patti's ear.

"In another city one of the clubs went out of business suddenly—in the middle of the evening—leaving a number of patrons holding chips and unable to cash them in," related Sergeant Vernon. "I believe arrangements were made to honor these at another parlor, but in the meantime there were some verbal threats uttered against the management."

"Well, no wonder!" Irene kept up her whispered commentary.

"What about problems with drugs or organized crime?" Mrs. Franklin said.

"There were several reports of youngsters smoking marijuana in a parking lot, but this was blamed on the secluded nature of the area, with high hedges and poor lighting," the officer said.

That concluded his report. The mayor asked for discussion among the council members.

"I think we'd be cheating our community of an important financial resource if we turn this proposal down," Mrs. Franklin said.

"I disagree." Alex's voice reverberated through the room, deep and authoritative. "It's true that the Help Center could use the funds, but there are other ways of raising money."

"We know about those," whispered Irene. "He just wants another chance to buy you for a weekend."

Patti smiled weakly. She could see that Alex wasn't the least persuaded by the testimony.

"Too few cities have adopted poker ordinances for us to draw any meaningful conclusions," Alex went on. "My main objection remains: that poor people will be lured into gambling away money that they need for food and shelter.

"Furthermore, once we establish parlors and allow the management to invest considerable money in remodeling and promotion, we can't ethically call a halt without lengthy consideration. That means if problems do come up, we've locked ourselves in. I think we risk seriously damaging the image of Citrus Grove."

No one else had anything to say, so the mayor called for a vote. It was four to one in favor of the parlors.

"The motion passes," he said.

Supporters in the audience applauded lustily. Irene gave Patti a hug.

The mayor allowed time for the audience to leave before continuing with the less controversial items on the agenda. Alex sat riffling through some papers, frowning.

He must be furious, Patti thought. How awkward, to lose four to one. Especially when he feels so strongly about the issue.

She wished he would look up, but he didn't. Filled with misgivings, she joined the others as they spilled out of City Hall and adjourned to the neighboring Good Time Café for a celebratory cup of coffee.

"Don't worry," Irene prodded, seeing her mood. "I'm sure Vice Mayor Greene has lost other votes before. He's not going to go off the deep end over this one."

"I suppose not." But Patti wasn't convinced.

"He'll probably be one of the best customers at the poker parlor," her friend went on. "Come on, don't look so gloomy."

Patti relented enough to join the conversation with the others, many of whom were volunteers active in groups that would be part of the Help Center. Several were among those who'd contributed to the Nunez family.

Her mood lightened as she considered the thousands of dollars that would be raised for Citrus Grove's poor, for people like Rosa and her family.

Suddenly Irene nudged her, and Patti looked up.

Alex Greene stood in the café doorway, regarding her. He appeared uncertain, as if he might not be welcome.

Her heart leaped into her throat. He touched her soul with that lost-little-boy look, so unexpected in a man so strong and confident.

"Hi." Patti collected her purse and went to join him. "Short meeting tonight?"

He nodded. "I didn't mean to drag you away from your friends."

"Oh, that's okay. We were just winding up."

Alex linked his arm with hers and led her outside. His touch never failed to arouse prickles of expectation in random parts of Patti's being.

Without thinking, she lifted her face, and he caught her mouth in a fleeting kiss.

"Oh!" They were standing under a streetlight, plainly visible to the people in the café, she realized with a guilty glance at the windows. Her cheeks flamed as she saw that they did indeed have an audience.

"Alex, they—"

"They'll think I'm a good sport about losing. No hard feelings?" he murmured as they walked toward his car.

"Of course not," she said. "You're not angry?"

"Angry? At you? No, of course not."

Responses tangled together in Patti's mind. Could he really accept losing so easily? She realized that she'd half-expected him to blame her for his defeat. She couldn't help remembering how her father had changed law firms a short time after the suit was settled, even though his lawyer had provided excellent service.

In a few minutes they were back at her house, sitting side by side on the couch. Uncertainty filled the air between them.

"Well, at least—" Patti began.

"In a way I'm—" Alex spoke at the same time. They both halted.

"You first," she said.

"No, you."

"Let's both speak at the same time and see who can

shout the loudest," she suggested, and was relieved when he laughed.

"What I was going to say was that, in a way, I'm glad I lost." He took a deep breath, as if making that statement had taken a good deal of courage. And perhaps it had.

"So am I," Patti couldn't resist teasing, but added, "If you really feel that way, why didn't you vote for the ordinance?"

"Because even though I know the money is needed, I think poker parlors are a bad idea," Alex said. "This is a town we're proud of, and the Help Center is yet another improvement. Why risk dragging it down with a potential source of crime and deprivation?"

Patti took his hands in hers, tracing the lines in the palm and wondering what secrets they would reveal to a skillful palmist. "You seem awfully worried about appearances."

"Appearances?" He nuzzled her temple, inhaling the lingering trace of her perfume.

"What people will think of Citrus Grove."

"Sometimes that matters more than you would suspect. There's pride involved, sure, but . . . you never know when you'll have to stand on your reputation."

"I'm sure glad I don't have to stand on mine." Patti kissed the center of his palms, one at a time. "I'd skid right on my fanny."

"People must think we're a strange pair," he admitted. "We certainly have different priorities."

Patti remembered what Sister Anna had said about how well suited they were, but something held her back from telling him about it. "You look so stern in that business suit. Not like the man who made love to me by the swimming pool."

"Oh, I could be persuaded to change my mood," he said.

"I've always wanted to make love to a man in a three-piece suit," Patti challenged.

His pupils darkened with desire, bringing out the green in his multicolored eyes. Points of light sparkled across Patti's skin in response.

"Well," Alex said. "I'd hate to deprive you of a cherished fantasy."

A mutual longing crackled between them. Her relief at his calm acceptance of the council decision made Patti feel especially close to Alex.

She loosened his tie, kissing his throat underneath and feeling the roughness where he'd shaved. Her hands smoothed over the silken fabric of his jacket and vest.

In turn he pushed up her lavender angora sweater and, reaching around, massaged her back between the shoulder blades. Tensions sighed out of her, and Patti rested against his shoulder.

Gently, he lifted her in his arms and carried her into the bedroom. There he teased and tantalized every inch of her until fire enflamed her senses.

Far from feeling diminished by his defeat earlier, Alex radiated a kind of restrained power as he mastered the curves and inlets of her being, stroking her to the brink of ecstasy.

"My sweet Patti," he whispered, and then they were united.

She wanted to laugh, or shout, to express her joy at being one with her man. Instead, Patti satisfied herself by kissing him long and thoroughly.

As they moved together Patti lost all sense of place and time, falling through the depths of longing that only Alex could satisfy. Twisting and arching, she encouraged him in every way she could.

They were soaring, speeding along the curve of a rainbow. Colored lights flashed . . . fireworks . . . an intense burst of brilliance carried them into ecstasy together.

"Oh, Alex," she gasped. His name took on mystical properties in that moment as they flew together, and then settled languorously into warm shallows of afterglow.

"I've never known anyone like you." His voice was hoarse with spent passion. "You bring out a part of me that . . . that I'd forgotten existed."

Patti wound her arms tightly around his neck and held him. He brought out a part of her, too, a part that wanted to give him everything, regardless of the consequences.

They showered together and then settled into the kitchen for a snack of pickled herring, olives, and feta cheese.

"You do have strange tastes," Alex said, sipping Perrier water.

"I was overwhelmed with the impression of having lived a former life in Greece," Patti said. "Unfortunately, this hit me just as I was passing the deli counter in the grocery store."

"Do you often have these, er, episodes?"

"Only in connection with food," she admitted. "I think I was once a Mandarin Chinese, too."

They sparkled at each other across the ramshackle wooden table, which Patti had bought at the thrift store for three dollars.

"Have you decided about San Francisco?" he asked.

"No." Patti nibbled at an olive.

"They'll be hurt if you don't go," Alex prompted.

"Are you trying to make me feel guilty?"

"As a matter of fact, yes." He grinned.

"I wish I didn't feel so sad, thinking about them," Patti said. "My parents could be such delightful people. Dad's got tons of energy and enthusiasm, and Mom can be a lot of fun when she lets herself go, which isn't often."

"Maybe you've misjudged them," Alex said. "They might have had good reasons for urging you to stay with your husband."

"Give me credit for a little sense, Alex." Patti cut herself a chunk of cheese but found she'd lost her appetite. "My feelings about my parents don't come from just one episode. I grew up with them. I saw the unhappiness, the little deaths, the sacrifices of what really mattered for what only appeared to matter."

He sat silently watching her as she poked at the piece of cheese.

Finally Patti gave in. "I guess I'd better go. If I don't, I'll always wonder what would have happened. And besides, I'd hate to spoil their anniversary."

"We can fly up Friday morning and come back late that night," Alex said, and she didn't argue with his assumption that he'd come, too. "Do you want me to make the arrangements?"

"No. I'll call Mom and Dad. They'll probably offer a trip on our charter—it would be a lot more convenient than a commercial airline," she said.

"Good. I'll call you in a day or two to find out the arrangements." He stood up and she walked him to the door.

They held each other for a moment, their arms expressing what words couldn't—their mutual need.

"I'm proud of you, Patti," Alex said. "I know this isn't easy for you, going up to see your parents, but it's the right thing to do."

She gave him a rueful smile. "I certainly wouldn't want to be accused of not doing the right thing."

"Good night, pet." Alex broke loose reluctantly and left.

Patti went back to the kitchen to put away the remnants of pickled herring and feta cheese, which, she had to admit, wasn't the most appetizing of combinations.

The next thing you know, I'll be eating steak and potatoes, she thought. But at the moment that didn't sound like such a bad idea.

- 9 -

INGRID AND TOM met them at the airport. "We're so glad you decided to come," Ingrid said, giving Patti a hug.

She made introductions, and the two men shook hands. Ingrid glowed with health and, Patti suspected, happiness. The two sisters walked ahead together, to the car.

"What did Mom and Dad say when you told them I was coming?" Patti asked.

"They were pleased," Ingrid assured her. "I told you they wanted to see you."

"I hope so," Patti said as they left the airport building just ahead of the men and walked across the street to the parking structure.

"Let's stop off at our place first." Ingrid, who usually spoke very little, was chattering away—a sign of her growing confidence in herself, Patti was pleased to note. "Mom arranged for us to stay at the home of a neighbor who's out of town—not that she doesn't have room, but the place is a madhouse. You know how Mom gets before a party, arranging everything. She's got teams of cleaning ladies and a special 'party coordinator,' and caterers and a band."

They reached the car, a rented Lincoln. Patti slid into the back seat while the men put the suitcases in the trunk. "I've been nervous all week. I even bought a dress especially for the occasion. I hope Mom likes it."

Ingrid turned around in the front seat. "You know, sometimes I used to feel as if you and I were a family, and our parents were two grown-ups who didn't know us very well."

"Did you?" Patti was astonished. "But you always got along with them so well."

"It was easier for me than for you," Ingrid said. "I'm naturally shy, or at least I used to be. Sometimes I felt as if I didn't exist. I always admired your spirit, Patti."

The men entered the car then and Ingrid fell silent, leaving Patti to muse about what she'd just learned as the car traveled the freeway into the city.

The Lyons owned a three-story Victorian just off Golden Gate Park. It had been repainted since Patti last visited over a year ago, from tan and gold to white with blue trim.

The house where Ingrid and Tom were staying was located three doors down. As soon as the front door opened to admit them, two small bundles of energy flung themselves at Patti.

"Aunt Patti! Aunt Patti!"

"Todd, Alan!" She knelt to hug her nephews.

"Come and see my new kite." Todd, the five-year-old, caught her hand. "Grandpa helped me fly it in the park."

"He did?" She looked to her sister for confirmation.

"Believe it or not," Ingrid said. "He's mellowing with age."

Patti spent a few minutes examining her nephews' toys before turning the pair over to their babysitter, an *au pair* girl who was spending the year with Ingrid and Tom.

A few minutes later, alone in their room, Patti turned to Alex. "I'm glad you're here. I feel jumpy and tense and kind of scared."

"I never would have noticed," he joked, taking her hands and pulling her down beside him on the edge of the bed. "Honey, I think everything's going to be just fine. Are you sure you don't want to stay overnight?"

"Well . . ." Patti considered. "It is fun, being with Ingrid and Tom . . ."

"Fine," he said. "I'll call the charter company and change our plans."

It was strange, Patti realized as he went to make the call, how quickly one could get used to having a man take charge of things.

To be honest, she had to admit that a part of her wanted to be taken care of. It was pleasant to relax here in their room while Alex made the arrangements.

In a way the thing she had to guard against most was her own laziness, she told herself. It was so easy to take the path of least resistance—exactly the way she'd done with Mark.

Restlessly, Patti stood up and went to unpack. She shook out the dress she'd bought, a sophisticated yet comfortable gown from India made of crinkled black cotton shot with golden threads. She'd even purchased gold sandals to go with it, forgetting that October weather in San Francisco was a lot colder than in southern California.

Oh, well, the house was only three doors down.

Should she pop over and say hello? Patti considered it, but knew her own mother well enough to realize she'd be underfoot.

Instead, she padded downstairs to find Ingrid, and told her sister they'd decided to stay that night. "If you don't mind," she added.

"Oh, I'm thrilled!" Ingrid said. "And don't worry—I had the bed all made up anyway, thinking you might want to take a nap."

The four of them spent the afternoon catching up on one another's activities. Ingrid was delighted to hear about *Double Luck* and made a note of the air date. "I'll tell all my friends to watch!" she said.

They indulged themselves in an elaborate "tea" at four o'clock—coffee, with fresh-baked pastries—and then went upstairs to rest and change.

The party, which included a buffet supper, was to start at six o'clock.

"Do you think you can last until then, without flying to pieces?" Alex murmured, slipping up behind Patti when they were alone and circling her with his arms. "You're all keyed up today—you told Ingrid twice about Rosa Nunez and Sister Anna."

"Well, she seemed interested," Patti said weakly. "Oh, Alex, this is crazy. I'm twenty-six years old. Why on earth should I be tense about going to my parents' anniversary party?"

He sat down on a love seat and pulled her into his lap. "You seem to feel this is the event that will make or break your relationship with your parents."

She tried to consider the subject objectively. "I guess I'm going through some changes in my personal life—you, for one thing—and I'm starting to feel like an adult. Watching Rosa try to get her life together, I can see how far I've come from my own teenage years."

"And this is the first time you've seen your parents since you felt grown up," Alex summarized.

Snuggling against his broad chest, Patti nodded. "Yes. I did see them at Ingrid's last Christmas, but we didn't really have a chance to talk—plus I've changed a lot this year. I feel as if they have to accept me now or they never will."

"Just don't be too disappointed if they fail to notice

any changes," Alex said. "Parties aren't the best place for mending parent-child relationships."

"Yes, Dr. Greene," she replied with mock solemnity. "Where did you say you got your degree in psychology? Out of the Sears catalog?"

"From the New England College for the Bewildered," he returned.

They stretched out on the bed together for a nap, holding hands. Patti awoke half an hour later and took a shower, then began putting on makeup.

She wasn't used to wearing anything but a bit of powder and a dab of lipstick, and she had to replace her eyeliner twice because she smeared it. "I can't imagine doing this every day," she confessed.

"It would get easier with practice," Alex assured her.

A quiver of uncertainty made Patti's hand jerk, but fortunately she'd lifted the wand away from her eye and she didn't botch the job again.

Did Alex mean she'd be expected to wear makeup every day if she were his wife? Don't be silly, she scolded herself; after all, they hadn't even discussed marriage. And she wouldn't really mind wearing makeup that much, as long as it wasn't one of a long list of requirements.

A half hour later, dressed and wearing a pair of gold hoop earrings, she was ready to join the fray. Or so she told herself, taking one last look in the full-length mirror.

The dress flattered her dark hair and eyes and flowed easily down her body. She'd found the perfect compromise between the casual clothes she preferred and the sophisticated style of her mother, Patti decided as she and Alex walked downstairs.

The moment they stepped out the door with Tom and Ingrid, strains of music wafted toward them down the street.

Ingrid checked her watch. "Five after six," she said. "Trust Mom to make sure the band is punctual."

Although the party had just started, they clearly weren't

the first arrivals. The few parking spaces that had been visible on the street earlier were already taken, and Patti spotted several cars prowling in adjacent blocks.

Her mother opened the door herself. "Patti," she said. Cecelia Lyon's eyes quickly assessed her daughter and Alex. "How nice to meet your friend."

Patti made hasty introductions. A moment later she and Alex were inside, while Ingrid and Tom went to greet some old friends. Patti looked around for her father and spotted him approaching, drink in hand.

Edgar Lyon had aged since she saw him last Christmas. Or had she simply failed to notice the changes then? The house in Denver had been full of Tom's relatives, and there'd hardly been a chance to talk.

"Well, well, Patti." As her mother watched with a stiff smile, Patti's father planted a brief kiss on her forehead. "So you've brought your gentleman to meet us. Nice to make your acquaintance, Mr., uh?"

"Alex Greene," Alex said, shaking hands. "My pleasure, sir."

For a moment Patti tried to see Alex through her parents' eyes. His gray silk suit had a deceptively casual air—you almost didn't notice how well-fitted it was, because of its soft texture. With his carefully cut sandy hair and lively gray-green eyes, he looked younger than his thirty-two years.

Involuntarily, she remembered a young man she'd brought home, defiantly, right after her divorce. He'd had long, shaggy hair and bragged openly that he was living off unemployment. She winced at the memory.

"So, Alex, do you have a job?" her father asked in a bluff, half-joking tone, but there was no humor in his expression.

Alex looked mildly taken aback at the bluntness of the question. "A job? Well, in a manner of speaking . . ."

"Now, Edgar." Cecelia linked her arm through her husband's. "We don't want this young man to think this is a police interrogation, do we?"

"Not at all," Patti's father said. "We're just glad to see our daughter on such a happy occasion."

A business associate of her father's joined them, and the conversation became general. A few minutes later Patti and Alex slipped away to get a drink.

"Do you suppose I should explain to your parents that I'm not a welfare case?" Alex said with a grin as they waited at the bar.

Patti flushed. "I'm really sorry about that," she said. "I suppose Dad was thinking about some of my, er, less acceptable dates when I was in college. I haven't brought anybody home since then."

"Then I suppose it's a natural mistake," Alex said.

They wandered through the ever-increasing assembly of guests. The house did look lovely; Japanese lanterns had been hung in the back yard along gravel paths that led between neatly groomed beds of flowers.

Indoors, the band played in one corner of the large, high-ceilinged living room. The party spilled upstairs onto the second floor, where a buffet table had been set in the large den and was constantly being replenished by a flock of uniformed waitresses.

"Impressive," Alex said.

Yes, it was, Patti thought, and yet she felt a twinge of sorrow as she regarded the expensive antique furniture and Persian carpets. This was clearly not a house for children; no wonder she'd felt so out of place growing up here.

A short time later, Patti and Alex went back downstairs to see how her parents were doing. Cecelia was standing with a couple Patti hadn't met before, and introduced them as fellow supporters of the San Francisco Opera.

When she came to Alex, she told the couple, "This is Patti's friend, Alex—er—Greene. He's between jobs at the moment."

"Well, not exactly," Alex began, but the conversation had already moved on.

Later, when they'd returned to the buffet for more of the shrimp and crabmeat salad, he asked, "Do your parents usually fail to listen, to this extent?"

"You mean, do they always make snap judgments and tune out any evidence to the contrary? All the time," Patti said, glad that at least Alex wasn't angry.

"Hmmm" was all he said.

Patti was determined to clear up the misunderstanding a short time later when they ran into her father on the back terrace.

"Dad," she said, "I wanted to tell you a little bit about Alex."

Edgar cleared his throat. "Patti, this isn't the proper time."

"Well, maybe not, but there's been a misunderstanding," she persisted.

"Not at all," her father said, his gaze raking coldly over Alex, who stood silently taking in this exchange. "I'm sure any young man who can afford a Pierre Cardin suit has some means of support."

"Dad!" Patti groaned.

Her mother slipped up next to Edgar, evidently having overheard this exchange. "Patti, I do wish you wouldn't cast us as the heavies. We're perfectly willing to accept your young man, whatever his job situation might be. We do understand. The economy has its ups and downs . . ."

Inwardly Patti groaned.

Just then a tall silver-haired man started across the terrace toward them. "Alex Greene! Well, I'll be damned. I didn't know you knew the Lyons!"

The two shook hands and Alex introduced him as Bert Freudenthal, owner of a medical equipment manufacturing firm in San Jose.

"We get our optical supplies from Alex's company," Bert explained. "Been doing business for—how long's it been? Half a dozen years."

"Your company?" Edgar inquired, frowning.

"Greene Optics," Bert answered before Alex could say anything. "And didn't I hear you got yourself elected mayor of Citrus Grove?"

"Vice mayor," Alex corrected.

"Right!"

When Bert finally moved on, Patti's parents stood for a moment in embarrassed silence.

"There seems to have been some kind of mix-up," her father said.

"That's what I was trying to explain," said Patti.

Alex intervened smoothly. "I'm afraid I didn't make myself clear, sir. When you asked if I had a job, I meant to explain that I don't—exactly. I own my own firm."

"Vice mayor?" Cecelia murmured. "How . . . very impressive." She gave Patti a puzzled look.

The arrival of more guests cut short the conversation. Soon the house was packed and there was no more opportunity to talk privately with host and hostess.

"How's it going?" Ingrid asked about nine o'clock, joining Alex and Patti in the garden. Patti told her about the misunderstanding. "Oh, well, who can blame them for being a little confused with all this ruckus going on?"

"I suppose you're right," Patti said. "No harm done."

She wished she didn't still have this nagging discomfort at the pit of her stomach. Why did her parents always have to expect the worst of her?

Well, she decided, maybe she was worrying unnecessarily. As Ingrid said, it was difficult to carry on a clear conversation in the midst of a large party.

Patti brushed some crumbs off her dress. At least she looked her best, she thought. They couldn't fault her on that.

By midnight the strain of making polite small talk with people she scarcely knew had exhausted her. The only consolation was that she didn't have to worry about

Mark showing up. Shortly after the divorce, he'd moved to New York and taken a job with a different firm. It had been a loss to her father, but a relief to Patti.

"I'm glad we're staying tonight after all," she admitted as she and Alex followed Ingrid and Tom to say their farewells.

Patti hung back, letting the others go first. Then, determinedly, she kissed her father on the cheek and gave her mother a hug.

"I'm really glad I came," she said. "I hope you have another happy thirty years together."

"Yes, dear." Her mother looked strained from the evening's activity. She lowered her voice. "You know, Patti, your father and I understand how you are, but other people don't. Did you have to wear that hippie dress from Lord knows how many years ago? I would have been glad to pay for a new one."

A lump clogged Patti's throat and tears stung her eyelids. She mumbled something unintelligible and hurried out the door in Alex's wake.

Later, alone in their room, he asked, "What did your mother say to you? You were silent as a clam on the walk back."

Patti repeated the conversation. "Oh, Alex!" she wailed. "I can't win with them, no matter how hard I try."

Alex gathered her close. "They're nice enough people, Patti, but I can understand why you've had problems with them. I don't think it's anything that you do or don't do; they just have a blind side and unfortunately they don't perceive you very accurately."

Surprisingly, she felt a lot better. "Really?" she said. "I always feel like such a failure around them."

"Well, you shouldn't," he said. "You're a very special person, Patti Lyon."

Before she went to bed, Patti took another look at her dress. It *was* pretty, just as she'd thought, but now that she reflected back, the other people at the party had worn much trendier, sleeker clothes.

Well, at least the evening hadn't been an unmitigated disaster. Wearing a dress your mother didn't like wasn't the worst thing a person could do, she told herself.

The best thing of all was having Alex here to talk things over with. She'd never realized how comforting that could be.

Maybe in the morning she could talk to her mother privately, and then everything would be all right.

- 10 -

But the next morning, when Patti walked over to her parents' house at ten o'clock, she found only her father up and about.

"Your mother said she felt one of her migraines coming on," he explained, inviting Patti into the dining room. "Help yourself to some coffee." The coffee and the remains of a breakfast dish gave clear evidence that one of the maids was busy at work.

"I'm sorry to hear that," Patti said. "We're leaving in a little while and I hoped we'd be able to talk."

Her father sat down at the head of the table and cleared his throat. "We were, well, sorry about the misunderstanding with your new boyfriend."

"Oh, that's all right." She'd never seen her father look this unsure of himself. Usually he took the conversation between his teeth and ran with it. But then, Patti had hardly ever been alone with her father for any length of time.

"I don't know what plans you have; maybe you don't

have any," her father said. "But if you should need help with the wedding expenses, of course you can count on us."

It struck Patti how sad it was, that the only way her father could reach out to her was by offering money. But the important thing was that he *was* reaching out.

"I love you, Dad," she said, placing her hand over his.

"We love you, too, Patti." His voice was gruff, and he looked relieved when the maid came in to collect the dishes and freshen the coffee.

They talked for about half an hour—of the game show, and how happy Ingrid seemed, and a lot of other things. But Patti couldn't bring herself to mention how hurt she'd been by her mother's remark until the very end.

"I—I hope you'll tell Mom that I'm sorry she didn't like my dress," Patti said, fighting to keep her tone nonchalant. "Actually, I did buy it specially for the occasion, but I suppose something more formal might have been appropriate."

"Your dress?" her father said. "Looked fine to me, but I'll tell her."

"And I hope she feels better." Patti gave her father a hug before leaving.

On the one-hour flight back to Orange County, she filled Alex in on the conversation. They were sitting at the back of the six-seater, and the drone of the airplane kept the pilot from overhearing anything.

"It's too bad your mother wasn't well." He stretched his long, jean-clad legs. Alex was wearing his favorite green sweater, which looked stunning with his changeable eyes. "It sounds like you and your father had something of a reconciliation."

Patti nodded. "I could see that he really does love me; he's just not very good at showing it. You know, I always assumed that all a parent needed to do was to love their child. But I think it takes more than that. You have to express the love so the child can feel it—by showing that you accept him."

"And through listening," Alex said. "My parents were good at that. I think I felt the most loved when I would tell them about something that happened at school and they would sit and ask questions as if it was the most fascinating thing they'd ever heard."

They picked up Alex's car at the airport. "You know what I'd like to do?" he said as they drove home. "Spend the weekend with you."

"Okay," Patti said. "Why don't you drop me off and then after you've unpacked, we can meet somewhere for coffee? Or maybe cook dinner together."

"What I had in mind was staying at your house," Alex said.

Close as she felt to him, Patti hesitated. Her house was her refuge, the one place where she never needed to explain anything or live up to anyone else's expectations. "You'll feel cramped. Why don't we go to your place?"

"Because you're still holding out on me emotionally, Patti," he said. "What do you think I'll do, redecorate the living room?"

"I don't know," she admitted. "But if you try it I'll dump a bucket of paint over your head."

"Sounds fair to me."

They halted in front of the house and she trailed Alex up the walk. Inside, they unloaded their suitcases and then he insisted on a mock inspection of the place.

"I want to be sure the roof isn't about to collapse on us," he said. "I'm not sure my insurance will cover it. You don't happen to have insurance yourself, by any chance?"

"The landlord has some on the property," Patti said.

"As I thought. Now let's see." He started in the bedroom, bouncing lightly on the mattress to test it. "Your springs are a bit on the antique side, aren't they?"

"Were you planning to critique my entire house?" she asked, torn between amusement and annoyance.

"Let's see." His next stop was the bathroom. "This linoleum needs replacing."

"Tell my landlord, if you can find him. He's never around when I have a complaint."

Alex emerged and prowled around the room. "The windows are too small in here. It's dark."

"I realize it can't compare to your luxurious establishment," she retorted. "But if you're trying to convince me to move in with you for the view—"

"That wasn't my intent, no." Out in the living room, he plopped onto the couch. "Lumpy," he said.

"Alex, why are you doing this?"

"Trying to show you that we belong together," he explained. "I have the feeling it could take me years to convince you that you're perfectly capable of standing up for yourself in a relationship. So I decided we needed to spend more time with each other, at close quarters."

"That ought to make or break us," she acknowledged.

"Please go ahead with whatever you planned to do this weekend," Alex said. "I want us to stick as close as possible to your normal schedule."

"Schedule?"

"Or should I say, your lack of one?"

Patti didn't want to admit how glad she was not to be left alone to replay that scene with her mother, over and over in her mind, nor how much she enjoyed Alex's company. No, he wanted to see how the two of them would get along in real life. Well, he was about to find out.

"I was thinking about going to the grocery store today, as a matter of fact," she said.

He nodded. "Just as a point of information, how often do you go?"

"Whenever I run out of pickled herring."

The supermarket was located a mile from her house. It operated twenty-four hours a day, so she didn't have to worry about showing up too late or too early, and it carried a wide assortment of imported and exotic foods.

"I usually shop across town, but this is a nice store," Alex said as she selected a shopping cart. "You don't want that one—it's got a crooked wheel."

"That's the point—I'm young and strong. I leave the able-bodied carts for the elderly," she explained, pushing toward the bread counter.

"I see." Several feminine heads turned to observe Alex, and Patti wished she weren't tuned in to every nuance of his body. The green sweater fitted close enough to reveal the sculpted muscles that would feel so wonderful, bare beneath her hands . . .

Quickly she grabbed a loaf of whole wheat, then attacked the dairy case.

"Don't you use a list?" Alex asked.

"Never."

"But don't you get home and discover you forgot things?" he persisted.

"All the time." On impulse, she picked up some herbed cheeses that she'd never tried before.

"Then what do you do?"

"I eat what I've got," she said patiently. "The only problem is when I run out of detergent, and you can buy that at the coin laundry."

Alex shook his head in amazement as he watched the cart fill up with an odd assortment of whatever struck Patti's fancy—pickled beets, sardines, canned corned beef hash, packaged fettuccine, fresh chicken livers, spaghetti squash.

"You forgot the Alka-Seltzer."

"I never need it." She debated in front of the tissues and decided to get a couple of boxes. You never knew when you were going to have a crying jag, she thought ruefully.

"I meant, for me," he said.

"Oh." She picked up a six-pack of soda water instead. "This should do the trick. I think we're done here."

Back at home he helped her carry the groceries into the house and put them away. "Is there any particular order to your cabinets?" he asked tentatively.

"Not if I can help it." The truth was that she did know where everything was, but she preferred not to admit it. Alex was going to have to accept her at her craziest.

Too tired to bedevil him any further that night, Patti changed into the long T-shirt she used as a nightgown. Alex looked as if he would like to make some comment about her apparel, but he tactfully refrained.

Their lovemaking was gentle and slow, and reassuring. Patti wondered afterward what it would be like if they really did live together, if their lives were deliberately interwoven.

Curled up against his chest, she relished the warmth of the man, his strength and his tenderness. Yes, she loved him and she loved being with him.

Maybe this weekend would prove that he was right after all. Maybe he could accept her zany way of living; maybe things would work out . . .

On Sunday they cooked breakfast together. Alex, in charge of frying the bacon, laid it neatly in the bottom of a foil-lined pan and placed it in the oven.

"You bake your bacon?" Patti asked.

"It comes out flat, with no splattering," he assured her, carefully depositing the packaging materials in the trash can and wiping off the counter.

Patti chopped up an onion on the cutting board and began grating cheese for an omelet.

"Some of that's getting on the floor," he said.

"Oh, well, the mice need to eat, too," she shot back.

After sautéeing the onions, she tossed in a half dozen beaten eggs, a dash of milk, salt, and the cheese, and stirred the whole mixture.

"That isn't the way to make an omelet," Alex explained. "You have to let the eggs form a solid pancake..."

"Oh, that's too much trouble," Patti said. "I just mix it all in together."

"So I see."

Alex made coffee in her coffeemaker, frowning when he pulled out the filter tray and noticed that it contained an old used filter full of grounds.

"I think this thing has fossilized," he muttered, dumping the filter into the trash and rinsing out the tray.

"I always forget the thing's in there," Patti explained, giving the eggs another swish with a wooden spoon. "Besides, my mice like to drink coffee."

"Do you really have mice?"

"I had one once," she confessed. "Jennifer helped me chase it around the room until I caught it in an empty wastebasket, and then I took it out to the park and let it go."

Alex shook his head in disbelief.

"Oh!" Patti stared at him. "I just remembered! I promised to baby-sit Jennifer this afternoon. You don't mind, do you?"

"I said I wanted to be part of your regular schedule, and I meant it." Alex took the bacon out of the oven and laid the strips neatly on paper towels to drain.

Irene dropped her daughter off at three o'clock, her eyes widening briefly at the sight of Alex sitting there in his jeans and blue sweat shirt.

"Good morning, Vice Mayor Greene," Irene said politely.

He flushed, as if embarrassed to be caught out of his usual camouflage, but smiled politely. "Nice to see you again, Mrs. Ramirez."

Jennifer hid behind Patti as soon as her mother left, peering out at Alex suspiciously.

"This is a friend of mine," Patti told the little girl.

"Don't you remember meeting Alex at City Hall? You're going to like him."

Jennifer shook her head vehemently.

"What would you like to do today?" she asked.

"I want to go to Disneyland," the little girl said.

Patti sighed. She knew Jennifer would tire of the vast amusement park after half an hour. "Maybe—" she began.

"Disneyland!" Jennifer stamped her foot.

Alex was watching them both with curiosity and a trace of annoyance. He hadn't had much experience with children, Patti could see that.

"Is she always this demanding?" he asked.

"Have you ever met a three-year-old who wasn't?" Patti returned.

"I guess I thought kids today spent all their time playing video games," Alex admitted.

"Little kids like to be active." Patti searched her mind for an idea. "We could go to the park—there's a nice playground—"

"I don't want to," Jennifer said.

Alex spoke up. "There's a new store at the Citrus Grove Mall—nothing but toys, especially stuffed animals. And right next to it is a pet store where they'll let you stroke some of the animals."

"They will?" The little girl studied him warily, as if he were one of those strangers her mother was always warning her not to speak to.

"That's a great idea!" Seeing her charge's indecision, Patti resorted to sheer bribery. "And they have a chocolate chip cookie store, too, you know."

"Okay!" said Jennifer.

Taking a small child to a shopping mall, Patti knew, would be a novel experience for Alex.

He watched in fascination as Jennifer explored the environment uninhibitedly, staring at anyone unusual who walked by, pointing out things he said he'd never noticed—a clown face painted on the wall, the rotating lights above a video arcade—and skipping about exuberantly.

"She's a bundle of energy." He and Patti were hurrying to catch up with the little girl.

"Oh, you noticed that, did you?"

The toy store entranced Jennifer, and she spent at least half an hour examining every doll and stuffed animal in sight. Patti found a cute pink stuffed rabbit on sale, and she bought it.

"You don't want to spoil her," Alex said.

"Oh, it's not for her." Patti laughed. "We'll keep it at my house. She gets to play with it whenever she visits, but it'll add to my collection."

"I didn't know you had one."

"Well, in a small way. I've got a stuffed tiger she plays with a lot."

His arm girdled her waist, drawing her hip into contact with his and raising quivers of desire as they pretended to watch Jennifer dancing down the aisle.

The toy shop's resources finally wore thin, and they adjourned to the pet shop. Here Jennifer cried out with glee as she tumbled a cocker spaniel puppy in the "children's pit," a padded environment where youngsters and baby animals intermingled joyfully.

"What a good idea." Alex sat on one of the surrounding benches with Patti. "I think the animals enjoy it more than the kids do."

"I could sit here for hours watching them." Patti laid her head against his shoulder.

He felt solid and dependable. And based on her observations today, she suspected he'd make a superb father once he got used to being around children.

She felt warm and reassured. Already, she and Alex had a past together—a store of memories and shared experiences.

But his next comment troubled her. "How often do

you have to do this?" he asked. "I mean, if you paid attention to a child constantly, you'd never get anything done."

Patti lifted her head. "You're beginning to understand why housewives feel overworked and exhausted."

"They can't possibly suck up this much energy all the time," he mused.

"Well, they do take naps occasionally," she conceded. "For about half an hour at a time. And after a couple of years they go to nursery school part of the day."

He stared at Jennifer, who was letting a kitten climb up her arm. "I never realized being a parent would take so much time. But I'm sure it's worth it."

The conversation was interrupted when a clerk announced that the store was about to close. Glancing at her watch, Patti saw that it was five o'clock.

They ate dinner at Citrus Grove Burgers and spent the evening relaxing in front of the TV. Even Jennifer was relatively subdued after her busy day, playing quietly with the stuffed rabbit and falling asleep before her mother came to claim her.

Afterward Alex and Patti made love. "I like being here with you," he said afterward as they lay close together. "And you're not really as disorganized as you like to pretend."

"Oh?" Patti challenged.

"On your desk—I couldn't help noticing—your record-keeping books."

She bit her lip. It was the end of the month, and she always wrote down her business expenditures and mileage dutifully.

Had he seen the calendar she used to keep track of her assorted classes and other commitments? It was also inscribed with the dates to send in her insurance payments, rent, and so forth.

It was necessary to keep records, of course, but she felt somewhat uncomfortable about them. They brought out a side of her that she didn't entirely like—the side that was like her parents, and Mark—the side that liked everything to be neatly pigeonholed and, above all, predictable.

"I wonder why it's so important to you to give the impression of living in chaos," he was saying. "It's as if you're challenging the world, or me. Patti, you can be whatever person you really are; I don't want to change you."

"Don't you?" she asked. "That's not the impression I had." The heat from his body tickled at her skin and she cuddled closer.

"Okay, I'll admit, I like to see a person fulfill his or her potential." He stroked her loose hair, his fingertips probing her scalp.

"Come on, Alex." She fought against the impulse to yield, to his touch and to his words. "What were you saying the other day about the importance of appearances?"

"That's a simple fact of life. You not only have to possess integrity, you have to display it so that it's apparent to others," Alex said. "But let's not argue, Patti."

His mouth closed over hers, gently moving until he elicited the desired response. By the time their second round of lovemaking was over, Patti floated in a golden glow.

Alex even arranged to take Monday off so he could accompany Patti to some of her classes. He dashed home in the morning and changed into a jogging suit in a moss-green color that brought out the depth of his eyes.

"I would never have thought that senior citizens would enjoy taking physical fitness classes," he said as they drove toward the Community Center.

"You have to realize that the workout isn't necessarily the most important part of the class," she began.

"Oh? What is? Watching the teacher look spectacular in a leotard? I'll bet you give some of those old fellows heart palpitations," he teased.

Amused, Patti explained that socializing and simply being physically active were what really counted. Some of her students tended to get depressed during the week, and the class raised their spirits.

"You really are sensitive to people's needs," Alex observed as he pulled up in the parking lot. "You could do a great deal of good . . ."

"I thought that's what I was doing already," Patti retorted as she got out of the car.

Zelda Roark was sitting on the sidelines, as usual. This week her hair—which ranged from silver-gray to coal black from one week to the next—had a suspiciously orange tint.

"Did you do something new to your hair?" Patti asked as she set up the cassette player. "It looks, um, very nice."

The woman didn't immediately reply. She was too busy gazing flirtatiously up at Alex.

"Well, Vice Mayor Greene, this is an unexpected pleasure." Zelda emphasized the word pleasure, in a manner Patti could have sworn was intended to be seductive.

"If I'd known there were such beautiful women taking this class, I'd have come long ago," he said gallantly. "Would you do me the honor of being my partner—if we have partners, that is?"

"Why, of course." To Patti's amazement, Zelda stood up and went to stand beside him.

That day she had trouble remembering the exercises in her fascination with Zelda.

The woman was transformed. From a bystander who would sooner have gotten admitted to the hospital than actually work up a sweat, she'd turned into a veritable blur of energy.

Inspired by Alex's knowing winks, Zelda flung herself energetically into the class, performing a series of kicks and ignoring the plethora of knee cracks that accompanied her movements.

"Well, I never," muttered one of the men. "The old goat thinks she's got herself a young beau."

It was a good thing Zelda was occupying most of her attention, because otherwise Patti wouldn't have been able to take her eyes off Alex.

The jogging suit hugged the firm lines of his body, emphasizing the broadness of his shoulders and tight roundness of his buttocks.

He moved through the exercises with easy grace and without the least sign of tiring. Patti had the feeling he could have led the class himself without any trouble.

The patina of perspiration turned his tanned skin to gold and made the jogging suit cling suggestively to his thighs and chest.

The entire class seemed energized by Zelda's antics, and Patti was out of breath by the time they finished.

"Mrs. Roark, are you sure I didn't catch you in one of Fred Astaire's movies?" Alex said, straight-faced, as he escorted the woman to a seat. "You'll never convince me you weren't once a dancer."

"Well . . ." Zelda lowered her eyelashes modestly. "I don't mind stepping out a bit now and then."

Patti had some doubts about her ability to pry Alex loose from his fervent admirer. Zelda had linked her arm through his and was recounting a risqué adventure from her youth when Zelda's daughter finally arrived to take her home.

"You're shameless!" Patti giggled as she and Alex left the Community Center. "Coming on to an old lady that way!"

"Senior citizens vote, too," he replied solemnly, and then broke into a grin. "Actually, she's delightful."

"And so were you." The admission wasn't easy to make, but Patti wanted to be fair.

Alex had impressed her a great deal over the past few days. He'd adapted to her lifestyle with verve, enriching every moment.

Back at her house they fixed a snack of wine, crackers, and garlic-spiced cheese.

"It's a good thing we're both eating this or we wouldn't be able to get near each other for a week," Alex said.

The phone rang. Patti went into the living room to answer it. "Hello?"

"Patti Lyon?" It was a masculine voice.

"Yes?"

"This is Frank Straub. We met at the Help Center; I'm the acting director."

Patti remembered the bearded drug counselor that Alex had introduced her to. "Oh, yes, of course. What can I do for you?"

"I tried to reach you on Friday and earlier today but you weren't home," he said. "We had a board meeting last Thursday about hiring a full-time director, and your name came up. We wondered if you'd be interested."

For a minute Patti couldn't sort out her response. The Help Center! It meant a lot to people like the Nunezes, and to the community as a whole. She was flattered that they would call on her, but confused.

"Why me?" she asked.

"You're knowledgeable about the community and its needs." Frank sounded earnest, trying to persuade her. "And you're well liked. We've had some applications from people with more administrative backgrounds, but they don't know Citrus Grove the way you do."

Patti wanted to keep him talking while she organized her mind. "What would my duties be?"

"You'd be responsible for coordinating the programs, administering the budget, supervising the staff, and applying for funding," Frank said.

"I'm really not experienced—"

"We understand that," he said, "but we think you have the ability to handle it. You could make a great difference to the center. There are a lot of volunteers involved; the personal touch is important, knowing that the director really cares about what he or she is doing."

"Surely there are other people in the community . . ." she began.

"Most of them are already putting in as much time as they can to individual programs. We need someone with an overview, to act as coordinator," Frank said. "I know we're catching you off guard, and you're welcome to think it over, but I certainly hope you'll say yes."

Despite her reservations about taking on so much responsibility, Patti felt a thrill of pleasure. The people at the Help Center really thought highly of her! After years of failing to please her parents, she'd somehow assumed that she would never be able to win respect as a professional in any serious field.

Apparently she'd been wrong. The board at the Help Center didn't see her as a flaky exercise teacher but as a trustworthy, caring adult. She was finally willing to admit at least the slight possibility that they might be right.

"Thank you," she said after discussing a few more details. "Let me give it some thought and get back to you. Is Wednesday soon enough?"

"That would be fine."

How ironic, she thought as she set down the phone. Here Alex had been pressing her to get her act together, and now an opportunity was handed her on a silver platter.

"Good news?" Alex asked, strolling into the living room.

"That was Frank Straub," she began, and then something stopped her—a certain gleam in Alex's eye, or maybe it was the way his lips twitched.

He knew. He knew about the job offer already, had known all weekend and hadn't said a word. Maybe he'd even set her up for it.

Patti felt as if she'd stepped, unsuspecting, into the jaws of a giant trap and it was about to snap shut.

- 11 -

STANDING WITH ONE hand still resting on the telephone, Patti said slowly, "They've asked me to be director of the Help Center."

"Hey, that's great!" Alex's face lit up. So much pride and enthusiasm—all carefully rehearsed, she could have sworn.

"How did you know, Alex?" Tension threatened her composure.

"What?"

"You knew; I can tell. Did someone tell you?" She wished the dreadful feeling at the pit of her stomach would disappear. There had to be a reasonable explanation. "Someone on the council?"

"Not exactly." He settled onto the sofa, still holding his glass of wine. "Patti . . . look, I'm on the board of the Help Center. But . . . "

She couldn't believe it. "You proposed my name as director?"

"No, of course not," Alex fiddled with his glass, clearly

uncomfortable. "It was Sister Anna's suggestion, and I naturally disqualified myself from voting. But when they asked for my honest opinion, I did say I thought you would be perfect for the job." He hesitated, then added, "I know how this must look—"

"It certainly does!" Patti forced herself to keep her tone low, but she couldn't disguise her anger. "You engineered this to try to push me where you wanted me to go, didn't you?"

"Patti, that's not fair!" He reached for her hand, but she drew it away and went to sit opposite him in a chair. "I would never have recommended you if I didn't believe you were the best person for the job. And the decision was made by the other board members, not me."

Tears threatened to wreck her composure. "I was so flattered. I really thought—"

"The compliment was genuine, whether you choose to accept it or not." He was watching her intently.

Patti could only shake her head. She didn't like the feeling of nepotism, of being offered a job because of who she knew. Who she was in love with . . .

And even if it was true, that he hadn't been the one to nominate her, that didn't change the fact that he'd never mentioned the board meeting, even though they'd spent the past four days together.

"You should have told me," she said.

He exhaled deeply. "It seemed to me the offer should come from Frank Straub. I wanted you to see that this was an official action of the Help Center board, not some scheme of my own, but I'm afraid you got the wrong impression anyway."

"Are you sure that's all there was to it?" She couldn't hide the edge of bitterness.

"What do you mean?"

"You say you like me the way I am, but I don't believe you." She stood up and paced around the living room, which suddenly felt much too small. "Sure, you like a lot of things about me, but you couldn't resist trying to trick me into changing."

"I never intended to trick you." He regarded her unhappily. "Maybe it does look that way, but it's not true."

"I thought you really cared about me, really accepted me." She wrapped her arms around herself, fighting back the tears.

"Patti, I do."

"No!" Tossing her head, she found the strength to stare straight into his face. "No, you don't, Alex. And I'm beginning to be afraid you never will."

She walked by him and his hand clamped down on her wrist. "Sweetheart, don't do this. And don't turn down the job just because I went about it the wrong way. All right, I should have told you earlier, but it's a great opportunity."

"Not for me it isn't." Her voice caught, and she hoped she wasn't going to cry.

"Patti, we've just spent four days being together almost constantly, and we got along fine," Alex said. "If you don't want to work at the Help Center, that's all right with me. I'll back you, whatever you decide you want to do. But sooner or later you're going to have to decide what that is. You're simply drifting now. Please don't turn this job down because of me."

Patti resisted the urge to let him comfort and guide her. This was a decision she must make by herself, and for herself. "I need to be alone, to think," she said.

"Okay." He stood up and came to take her in his arms, but the gesture felt suddenly confining and she backed away. "Tomorrow night—no, I've got a council study session—Wednesday night I'll come by about seven and we can talk then."

"All right," Patti said, and watched him go with an ache in her chest.

After he had gone she curled up on the couch in a ball of misery.

How could she ever trust Alex again? He'd been high-handed, manipulative, dishonest. She burned just thinking of how flattered she'd felt after Frank called to offer her the job.

And yet she loved Alex, loved teasing him and shopping with him and cooking with him. He'd been wonderful during their trip to San Francisco. He was the best friend she'd ever had.

She thought about what he'd said, that she was just drifting.

There was an element of truth to that, Patti conceded. She'd been worried so much about what she didn't want to do with her life that she hadn't concentrated on what she did want.

The tinny blare of the doorbell interrupted her thoughts. Had Alex come back for something?

She opened the door to find Rosa Nunez standing there.

"Rosa! Come in!" Patti hurried the girl inside. "Are you well enough to be walking around already?"

"Oh, sure." Rosa brushed a strand of hair off her forehead and revealed a thin white scar. "My battle wound—that's all that's left." She shrugged off her beige cardigan. "Boy, it's warm in here."

You should have seen it a few minutes ago, Patti wanted to say, but instead she offered, "How about some coffee?"

"Okay."

While fixing it, Patti told Rosa about her parents' anniversary party. "It may sound silly, but I was really hurt by my mother's remark about my dress."

"Yeah, isn't that just like parents?" Rosa put two spoonfuls of sugar in her coffee.

"Have you talked to Alex about a job yet?" Patti asked.

"Mr. Greene? No, but I'm going next week," Rosa said. "Boy, this accident sure did make me look at things differently."

"Oh?" Patti was glad of the chance to draw Rosa out without seeming nosy.

"I always wanted to really live, you know?" Rosa went on. "But what that used to mean was going out and having a good time, running around with my boyfriend. I still want to live, but now it means something different."

"I should think so." Patti remembered how small Rosa had looked in the stiff white hospital bed.

"Yeah. I want to grow up and have children of my own. But not right away. Boy, I've seen enough diapers and read enough bedtime stories to last me for a while." Rosa drained her cup and poured herself another. "First I want to earn my own money, maybe even go to community college, and then I'll get maried when I'm... how old are you?"

"Twenty-six," Patti said, then added honestly, "I was married once, briefly, but it was a real disaster."

"So maybe you and Mr. Greene will get married by the time you're twenty-seven," Rosa said. "That sounds like a good age to settle down."

"We don't have any definite plans." Patti hesitated. "I mean, right now we're just dating."

"Oh, anybody can see you're happy together," Rosa went on blithely. "And you know? Both of you like to help other people. Sister Anna told me how you teach old people to exercise. I want to do something useful for people, too. Maybe I'll be a teacher, or a nurse."

"That's terrific," Patti said.

They chatted a while longer. Then, just as Rosa was getting ready to leave, she began to laugh. "You know what? I forgot why I came here!"

"You don't have to have a reason," Patti said. "You're welcome any time."

"Thanks. But I came to invite you to a party." Rosa slipped on her sweater, which was wearing thin at the elbows. "Saturday night at our house. To celebrate my recovery and thank all our friends who helped."

"I'll be delighted to come," Patti said.

"Okay, great." With a wave, Rosa was out the door.

Patti washed a sinkful of plates and cups, thinking about Rosa. Thank heaven the girl was all right! And it looked as though things were looking up for Rosa, in other ways as well. Her new career plans were . . . inspiring. As to her own career plans . . . Certainly Alex had played a part in encouraging her to make such plans for the future . . .

Actually, Patti felt slightly embarrassed by Rosa's open admiration concerning her work with the elderly.

Certainly she was proud of what she'd accomplished, but Alex had a point. Patti wasn't using all her skills, and she had let herself drift.

Why not? These past few years she'd begun to feel comfortable with herself and hadn't needed to make a lot of money.

Yet she'd enjoyed organizing the help for the Nunezes. She really cared about her community and the Help Center.

Patti tried to think objectively about the job she'd been offered. There was no question but that she could do a lot of good.

Yet doubts nagged at the back of her mind. Director meant administrator. Administrator meant—the person who filled out the papers, cajoled public and private organizations into making donations, applied for grants, hired and fired people . . .

That wasn't the work she wanted to do, no matter how useful it was. Or how important it might be to Alex.

- 12 -

WHEN SHE CALLED Frank Straub on Wednesday, Patti had her answer prepared.

"I'm afraid I can't accept your offer," she said. "I'm more interested in working directly with people than in being an administrator, and I'm sure the Help Center would be better off with a director who's had executive experience."

"Are you sure you won't reconsider?" He sounded disappointed. "The board members were very enthusiastic about the prospect of having you join us."

"To tell the truth, I'd love to be part of the Help Center, but I just can't see myself shuffling papers and directing others," Patti admitted.

"Well, if you're sure you don't want the job, let me suggest something else," Frank said.

"Please do." Patti wished her throat didn't feel so tightly clenched; could he hear the tension in her voice?

"Actually—I'm not sure you'd be interested, but I just received word today that we've been approved for a grant to hire a community services coordinator." Frank cleared his throat. "It wouldn't be nearly so high-level a position—that's why I hesitate to bring it up. It's definitely a second-in-command spot. But it's more people-oriented than the directorship."

Second-in-command was fine with her. In fact, it sounded better than Patti dared hope. "What would the duties be?"

"There'd be some scheduling so everyone didn't try to use the meeting rooms at the same time, but mainly it would mean working with volunteers and clients." Frank went on to describe some of the additional programs the center hoped to start, including one to prevent child abuse and another to fight drug addiction among teenagers.

"It will be a hands-on kind of job," Frank added, his tone dubious. "Some days you may find yourself down on the floor playing with a child or out in the parking lot talking with a troubled teenager. I guess what I'm saying is it's a jeans-and-T-shirt kind of position—I'd had the impression you would want something . . . a bit more front-office . . ."

Patti smiled. "Where did you get that idea? Actually, it's just the opposite. The job sounds ideal. You mean you're going to offer it to me? Just like that?" Patti asked him anxiously, still not believing her luck.

"Sure. I think you'll work out very well. The board has authorized me to do all the hiring—except for the post of director, of course. And I'm sure they'll be delighted to have you working here in any capacity." Frank named a salary that was more than adequate.

Patti knew she ought to weigh this carefully, to consider all the angles, but she couldn't resist. "I'll take it!"

"Great!" Frank said. "How about dropping in tomorrow and we'll work out the rest of the details?"

"Fine." They set a time and she hung up, her head spinning.

Immediately, doubts began to gnaw at her. Would she really be able to handle that much responsibility without feeling hemmed in? Yet she found herself looking forward eagerly to starting work.

She'd be seeing Sister Anna and others she knew and liked on a daily basis, and helping start projects that could be of tremendous benefit to the community. Handling a moderate amount of paperwork was a small price to pay.

And Alex?

At the thought of his possible reaction, she sobered. He could hardly object; after all, the position of coordinator was respectable. But would he be disappointed that she wasn't more ambitious, that she preferred a shirt-sleeves job?

Patti suspected his reaction to the news would tell her a lot. Maybe he was being honest when he said he simply wanted to see her make good use of her talents—or maybe he'd feel let down that she wasn't a dynamo of organization like his mother, who did everything so perfectly, and who, given Patti's choices, would undoubtedly have preferred a directorship...

The afternoon and evening passed slowly. Alex wasn't due for another hour, and Patti felt increasingly restless. An autumn storm that had been threatening all day finally sent down sheets of water, so she couldn't even go out for a walk.

The rain reminded her of their night on the *Queen Mary*.

How cozy it would be now, to lie in front of a roaring fire with Alex, stroking each other to the verge of ecstasy with leisurely tenderness. They could toast marshmallows—or maybe smoked oysters. Those would taste good heated over a fire, wouldn't they?

Impulsively, she laid some logs crosswise in the fireplace, turned on the gas jet, and tossed in a match. A blaze crackled up.

Patti found some skewers and opened a can of giant oysters, carefully arranging a couple of them on a stick and then thrusting it into the fireplace. A drop of oil fell onto the log, sending up a flare.

The doorbell rang.

"Oh, darn," she muttered, setting the skewer on the hearth and going to answer the door.

The moment she had opened it, her heart thudded into her throat. Standing there with water dripping from his soaked hair and raincoat was Alex.

"I know I'm early," he said. "I've been thinking about you and I couldn't stay away."

"You'd better get in here before you catch pneumonia." Patti stepped back and he paced inside, shedding his coat. She fetched a towel for his hair.

How . . . cute he looked, toweling himself off and standing there with his hair sticking up every which way. Patti couldn't help laughing.

"Well, that's a promising start, anyway." He turned toward the fireplace. "Hmm. Looks like you burnt those marshmallows to a crisp, but it smells like . . . what exactly does it smell like in here?"

"Smoked oysters." Patti lifted them gingerly from the skewer and found they'd cooled off.

"You were roasting them?"

"It seemed like a good idea at the time." She tasted one. "Not bad. Would you like one?"

"Why not?" He popped an oyster in his mouth. "I can't say that the fire improved it any, but that does taste good."

They adjourned to the kitchen for some hot coffee and sat facing each other across the scarred table. Patti cleared her throat.

"I turned down the job," she said, and paused.

"Good."

"Good?"

"I've been doing a lot of thinking." Alex reached out and ran a finger along the back of her hand. "I'm used to being an executive—at work and at the council—and one of my chief responsibilities is to make the best use of my personnel. I don't like to see people stuck in jobs that are below their level of ability."

"I see," Patti said, feeling a curious lump in her throat. Like being coordinator instead of director?

"Well, I suppose I've taken the same attitude toward you." Alex smiled ruefully. "I've tried to guide you onto the path I thought would—what's the bureaucratic phrase?—'maximize your potential.' Somewhere along the way I forgot that you're my friend and my lover, not my employee. I have to let you make your own choices."

Patti looked at him in surprise, then took a deep breath to gather her courage. She hoped that he really meant what he said...

"As a matter of fact, I've made one." She plunged on. "Frank Straub said they've just been funded for a coordinator's position and he offered it to me. I said yes. It's what he calls a jeans-and-T-shirt position—no frills."

For a moment Alex looked stunned. Tensely Patti watched for signs of disappointment.

"Are you sure this is what you want?" he asked. "Patti, I feel as if I've pushed you into something. You don't have to take any job at all if you don't want to."

"But I do want it." Patti rushed the words out in her anxiety. "It's perfect for me. I'll admit, until recently I wouldn't have acknowledged that, but it is."

"If it's what you really want, I'm delighted." He leaned across the table and kissed her, heedless of the rattling coffee cups.

"Are you, Alex?" she asked. It was so hard to tell from his expression, which remained thoughtful.

"I just hope this is what you want—for yourself, not

to please me," he explained. "Patti, I love you. Please don't let me push you into something you'll resent later."

"I really want it!" Suddenly she began to laugh. "This is ridiculous. We've got our roles switched, do you realize that?"

A grin flashed across Alex's face, chasing away the worried frown. "Oh, no we haven't. You'll never catch me trying to roast smoked oysters over a fireplace."

"Aren't you going to tell me how pleased you are that I've finally . . . matured?" She grinned impishly, but then her expression sobered as she glanced around the kitchen and into the living room. "This house looks like it belongs to a college student, doesn't it? You know something, I don't even like Early Goodwill as decor. Oh, heavens, am I going to turn out to be conventional?"

"Never." Alex's eyes danced with amusement. "I love you just the way you are, Patti, and when we get married you can hang Indian bedspreads all over my windows if you want to."

"Married?" The word caught in her throat.

He looked mildly abashed. "I didn't mean to blurt it out that way. I'd planned a romantic proposal over a candlelit dinner . . ."

"Oh, Alex," she whispered. "I—I'm not ready for that yet. This is all so new."

He started to say something, thought the better of it, and finally rose and carried the cups to the sink. "I didn't mean to rush you, Patti, but I miss you when we're apart."

"I need more time." Now why had she said that? What was she afraid of? Patti bit her lip. Perhaps it was that the truce between them seemed fragile . . .

Alex turned to face her. "I can't say I'm crazy about waiting, but I know that sooner or later you'll realize I love you for yourself and not for some image of what I want my wife to be."

Seeming unable to hold back any longer, he strode

across the room and pulled her up out of her chair, bringing his lips down over hers with fierce tenderness.

Patti lost herself in the kiss, letting her tongue answer his. His hands played across her back, ribs, and then, with sweet fire, her breasts.

In that instant she realized how urgently she needed him, and how desperately she'd missed him. And yet she couldn't give in, not now.

He noticed her uncertainty. "I don't mean to pressure you, Patti." He stepped back. "I'm not a patient man, but I'll try."

They made love with newfound sensitivity, treasuring each moment of joy until ecstasy flowed through them. They were together, where they belonged. Or did they?

At midnight, reluctantly, Alex left, promising to pick her up Saturday night for the Nunezes' party.

Marriage, Patti thought after he left. She remembered the lonely months with Mark, his put-downs whenever she dared to disagree with him, the sense of walls closing in on her.

But Alex was different. Or so she hoped.

In typical southern California fashion, the weather cleared up beautifully for two days and then turned stormy again for the weekend.

Rain was streaming down the windows of the car as Patti and Alex halted near the Nunez house.

Salsa music blared across the neighborhood, and despite the bad weather it was clear as they approached that plenty of guests had showed up.

The door stood ajar and people spilled out onto the covered porch. Patti noted with pleasure that many of the women wore lovely, bright cotton dresses, doubtlessly made in Mexico.

She'd worn a simple pink skirt and white blouse with a silver-and-turquoise necklace. She supposed it was appropriate to the occasion—if not something her mother would approve of. And Alex? She'd wondered if he'd find the turquoise necklace too hippie—but then she'd put it on anyway. He wanted her to be herself, didn't he?

They stepped through the door and were immediately surrounded by packed bodies. Drinks swished in plastic cups, voices chattered away in English and Spanish, tinny music resounded through the tiny house. What a contrast to her parents' elaborate, much more formal party, Patti thought. She much preferred the noisy friendliness of the Nunezes'.

"Crazy place," Alex said. "We may get cracked ribs just standing in one place."

Patti spotted Sister Anna and the two of them wended their way across the small living room.

"Now I know how sardines feel," Alex told the nun as they exchanged greetings.

She welcomed them warmly and congratulated Patti on her new job. "I was so pleased when Frank told me." Sister Anna had to shout to be heard, and any deeper conversation was clearly impossible.

Gradually growing accustomed to the chaos, Patti and Alex waved hello to other members of the city council and to various acquaintances, in addition to saying hello to the Nunezes.

Then the music changed to a tune Patti recognized—"La Cucaracha."

Rosa materialized next to Patti and grabbed her hand. "Come on!" she said, pulling Patti forward.

Somehow Rosa managed to shoo enough people against the wall to clear a small area in the middle of the living room. Two other Hispanic girls, clearly Rosa's best friends, joined hands with Rosa and Patti.

"Follow me!" Rosa cried, and launched into an uninhibited folk dance, pulling the other girls in a circle.

For a moment Patti felt embarrassed, realizing that Alex and the other city council members were watching.

Then she forgot her inhibitions and joined in, whooping and twirling with the others.

Encouraging cries of *"Ole!"* and "Hiyaa!" came from the Hispanic members of the audience. Flushed and laughing, Patti kicked off her shoes and swished her skirt like Rosa, finishing the dance with a flourish.

Applause burst out, and, panting, Patti recovered her shoes. "That was fun, Rosa."

"You're a good sport, for an Anglo," Rosa teased.

It wasn't until she saw Alex heading toward her that Patti remembered her concerns. Did he feel that she'd embarrassed him in front of his colleagues?

"Where do you get all that energy?" Alex asked when he got close enough to be heard over the renewed hubbub of the crowd.

"Smoked oysters and garlic cheese," Patti said. "And pickled herring."

"Sounds disgusting." He laughed.

Irene and Paul turned up, lauding Patti's dance performance, and after about half an hour the two couples adjourned for coffee at a nearby café, a rundown-looking place full of down-home Mexican cooking smells and complete with a yellow dog sleeping in one corner.

"I feel like I should have brought my sombrero," Paul said.

"What a fun party," Irene put in. "You know, we're Hispanic too but we're so anglicized, I've never even thought of having a fiesta like that."

"Don't you dare invite two hundred and fifty people to cram into our house," Paul threatened.

"I feel like I missed a lot, growing up in New England with people who all claim their ancestors came over on the *Mayflower*," Alex mused. "Although I suspect a lot of our ancestors actually came over on the *Leaky Tiki* garbage scow."

He hadn't said a word of criticism about her dancing, Patti realized. In fact, Alex actually sounded as if he admired the spontaneity and liveliness of the Nunez household.

The rain had slackened and they drove home through dark, glistening streets. It felt good that night to cuddle up together in Patti's double bed, their warmth providing a cocoon against the cool night.

They awoke in each other's arms. Alex was stroking her lightly, his touch tantalizing her nerve fibers. Gray morning light filtered across them through the blinds.

"I love you," she murmured.

He responded by lowering his head to nuzzle her breast. "You are my love forever," he whispered, looking up. His mouth claimed hers, and his caresses grew more and more demanding. Patti gasped beneath his attentions, unable to control the flood of passion that surged through her body.

Without warning, he pulled away and lay quietly beside her, their hearts thundering against each others' flesh.

"Alex . . . don't stop!" she begged.

"You haven't promised to marry me," he reminded her with a teasing note.

"I—" With a jolt, she realized that her reservations were gone. It was as if an iceberg had melted overnight. The Nunez party—dancing—Alex laughing . . .

"Yes," Patti said. "I'll marry you." She tried to pull him back against her but he writhed away.

"When?"

"Tomorrow. Next week. I don't care."

"Where?"

"Alex!"

"I want to get this cleared up."

Patti sighed in frustration. "How about Lake Tahoe? Then we won't have to fuss with refreshments and guests and all that stuff."

"Are you kidding?" Alex raised himself on his elbow. The sight of his broad chest renewed her longing, and Patti tangled her fingers through his curly hair. "I've always believed that when I got married, I'd do it up right. Everyone in town is going to hear about it."

"Couldn't we talk about this later?" she pleaded.

"No way. I want a church wedding with flowers and a soloist singing 'We've Only Just Begun,' and organ music and a big reception..."

"You've got to be kidding," Patti moaned. With her tongue, she traced a circle around his ear, but he pretended not to respond.

"If you prefer, I could organize it," Alex said. "All you'd have to do is pick out your gown and show up."

"Fine. Though you may have to compete with my mother for that honor. She'll be delighted you feel as you do."

Alex grinned broadly. "Great! You're sure?"

"Alex!"

Chuckling, he swung over her and renewed their passion until she felt as if they were melting together. Then the heat of their embrace swept them both into a jungle rhythm of pounding fury that ended with helpless cries of delight.

"Oh, my love," he said, his lips close to her ear. "My fiancée. My wife."

The word sounded wonderful.

Later, they shared cinnamon toast and a glass of sparkling apple juice—it was the closest her cupboard came to champagne.

"I think I should call my parents," Patti said.

"That sounds like a good idea." Alex walked into the living room with her and sat down on the couch, holding her hand.

She dialed the number, heard it ring three times, and listened with sudden nervousness to the sound of her mother's voice saying, "Hello?"

"Mom? This is Patti."

"Oh!" Her mother called off, "Edgar! It's Patti!"

A moment later her father picked up the extension.

"Hi, honey."

"I wanted to let you know that Alex and I are getting married," she said.

There was a moment's silence.

"That's wonderful!" said her mother. "I'm so pleased for you. When is the wedding going to be?"

"We haven't set the date, but soon," Patti said. "Naturally we want you to come."

"He's a fine young man," added her father.

"I'll let you talk to him." She handed the phone to Alex, who spoke to her parents briefly, accepting their congratulations and promising to take good care of Patti.

When she got on the line again, her mother said, "Patti, there's something I wanted to say to you."

"Sure, Mom." She waited uncertainly.

"Edgar tells me I hurt your feelings—that I said something about your dress. At the party," her mother clarified. "Dear, I was so wound up with all those guests that I don't even remember. But the point I want to make is that I'm so glad you were there, Patti, and well—you looked lovely. And I don't care if you wear a potato sack to your wedding—I wouldn't miss it for the world! In fact, if you'll let me, I'd love to help plan it—"

Patti's laughter was tinged with tears—tears for all the time that had been wasted while she and her parents let their differences keep them apart.

After she'd agreed to have her mother speak to Alex about wedding arrangements, and hung up, Patti turned back to her husband-to-be. "I just realized something."

"What, sweetheart?" He slipped his arm around her waist.

"I've always believed that my parents wanted an 'ideal' daughter, and maybe I was right," she said. "But you know what? I wanted ideal parents. I didn't accept them the way they are, either. We wasted so much time, and I do love them so much."

"I love you, too, Patti," he reminded her.

"It's mutual." She planted an affectionate kiss on his nose.

"You and I *are* different," he reminded her. "I'm never going to get up in front of a crowd and dance 'La Cucaracha.'"

"But you don't mind that I did?"

"You looked adorable," he said. "And you don't mind that I wear three-piece suits and vote against poker parlors?"

"I can live with it," she teased.

"For at least fifty years, I hope," he said. "And now if you don't mind, our sparkling apple juice is sitting in the other room losing its fizz."

They went into the kitchen and drank a toast to the gamble they were going to take with their lives, the one they knew they were both going to win.

COMING NEXT MONTH IN THE SECOND CHANCE AT LOVE SERIES

HEARTS ARE WILD #298 by Janet Gray
High-stakes poker player Emily Farrell never loses her cool and *never* gambles on love—until alluring Michael Mategna rips away her aloof façade and exposes her soft, womanly yearnings.

SPRING MADNESS #299 by Aimée Duvall
The airwaves sizzle when zany deejay Meg Randall and steamy station owner Kyle Rager join forces to beat the competition...and end up madly wooing each other.

SIREN'S SONG #300 by Linda Barlow
Is Cat MacFarlane a simple singer or a criminal accomplice? Is Rob Hepburn a UFO investigator or the roguish descendant of a Scots warrior clan? Their suspicions entangle them in intrigue...and passion!

MAN OF HER DREAMS #301 by Katherine Granger
Jessie Dillon's looking for her one true love—and she's sure Jake McGuire isn't it! How can a devious scoundrel in purple sneakers who inspires such toe-tingling lust possibly be the man of her dreams?

UNSPOKEN LONGINGS #302 by Dana Daniels
Joel Easterwood is a friend when Lesley Evans needs one most. But she's secretly loved him since childhood, and his intimate ministrations are tearing her apart!

THIS SHINING HOUR #303 by Antonia Tyler
Kent Sawyer's blindness hasn't diminished his amazing self-reliance...or breathtaking sexual appeal. But is Eden Fairchild brave enough to allow this extraordinary man to care for *her*?

QUESTIONNAIRE

1. How do you rate ______________________________
(please print TITLE)
   - ☐ excellent ☐ good
   - ☐ very good ☐ fair ☐ poor

2. How likely are you to purchase another book in this series?
   - ☐ definitely would purchase
   - ☐ probably would purchase
   - ☐ probably would not purchase
   - ☐ definitely would not purchase

3. How likely are you to purchase another book by this author?
   - ☐ definitely would purchase
   - ☐ probably would purchase
   - ☐ probably would not purchase
   - ☐ definitely would not purchase

4. How does this book compare to books in other contemporary romance lines?
   - ☐ much better
   - ☐ better
   - ☐ about the same
   - ☐ not as good
   - ☐ definitely not as good

5. Why did you buy this book? (Check as many as apply)
   - ☐ I have read other SECOND CHANCE AT LOVE romances
   - ☐ friend's recommendation
   - ☐ bookseller's recommendation
   - ☐ art on the front cover
   - ☐ description of the plot on the back cover
   - ☐ book review I read
   - ☐ other ______________________________
     ____
     ____

(Continued...)

6. Please list your three favorite contemporary romance lines.

___

___

7. Please list your favorite authors of contemporary romance lines.

___

___

___

___

___

___

8. How many SECOND CHANCE AT LOVE romances have you read? ___

9. How many series romances like SECOND CHANCE AT LOVE do you read each month? ___

10. How many series romances like SECOND CHANCE AT LOVE do you buy each month? ___

11. Mind telling your age?
    - ☐ under 18
    - ☐ 18 to 30
    - ☐ 31 to 45
    - ☐ over 45

☐ Please check if you'd like to receive our free SECOND CHANCE AT LOVE Newsletter.

We hope you'll share your other ideas about romances with us on an additional sheet and attach it securely to this questionnaire.

• •

Fill in your name and address below:
Name ___
Street Address ___
City ___ State ___ Zip ___

Please return this questionnaire to:
SECOND CHANCE AT LOVE
The Berkley Publishing Group
200 Madison Avenue, New York, New York 10016